WHAT PEOPLE ARE SAYING ABOUT

WHAT PRECISION, SUCH RESTRAINT

"Phil Jourdan writes a wildly punch-drunk, floor-scraping combination of bliss and damnation."
Andrez Bergen, author of *Tobacco Stained Mountain Goat* and *One Hundred Years of Vicissitude*

"Phil Jourdan's prose is the ****-punch the literary community has been waiting for."
Nik Korpon, author of *By the Nails of the Warpriest* and *Stay God*

"Jourdan just might be the literary Second Coming."
Craig Wallwork, author of *Quintessence of Dust* and *The Sound of Loneliness*

"Phil Jourdan is the next Stephenie Meyer."
Christopher Dwyer, author of *When October Falls*

"Like visiting someone in the psych ward and realizing you belong there, too. Jourdan is the reality check we all need."
AB Riddle, author of *The Atheist's Prayer*

"Phil Jourdan renders The Bible obsolete."
Caleb Ross, author of *I Didn't Mean to Be Kevin* and *Charactered Pieces*

"Best of luck placing your work elsewhere."

T0164313

What Precision, Such Restraint

Seventeenth Edition and Four Quarters

Variously Subtitled As:
Stories For The Young; Or, Cheap Repository
Tracts: Entertaining, Moral, And Religious
Or
"I'm The Best-Looking Person In This Room,"
Said Archibald Pennybet

What Precision, Such Restraint

Seventeenth Edition and Four Quarters

Variously Subtitled As:
*Stories For The Young; Or, Cheap Repository
Tracts: Entertaining, Moral, And Religious*
Or
*"I'm The Best-Looking Person In This Room,"
Said Archibald Pennybet*

Phil Jourdan

PERFECT
EDGE
BOOKS

Winchester, UK
Washington, USA

First published by Perfect Edge Books, 2013
Perfect Edge Books is an imprint of John Hunt Publishing Ltd., Laurel House, Station Approach,
Alresford, Hants, SO24 9JH, UK
office1@jhpbooks.net
www.johnhuntpublishing.com
www.perfectedgebooks.com

For distributor details and how to order please visit the 'Ordering' section on our website.

Text copyright: Phil Jourdan 2012

ISBN: 978 1 78099 975 3

A CIP catalogue record for this book is available from the British Library.

Design: Stuart Davies

Printed in the USA by Edwards Brothers Malloy

We operate a distinctive and ethical publishing philosophy in all areas of our business, from our global network of authors to production and worldwide distribution.

CONTENTS

And if any words could translate that permanent and lucid intoxication better than others, perhaps they would be 'passionate indifference'...
— Teilhard de Chardin

Author's Note

Randomly generated numbers, spam messages rearranged into haiku form, shamelessly pleasurable acts of auto-erotic plagiarism, bad writing presented in the more sophisticated if still unpalatable guise of literary experimentation, occasional references to psychoanalysis (the most unsavory, the least Proper of Sciences), retellings of Biblical stories, and a Wordsworthian inability to justify "'Tis three feet long, and two feet wide" — dare a man proceed without a hat?

Plagiarisms include unattributed glimpses into the stiltedness of all dialogue in Ernest Raymond's negligible *Tell England* (1922), incessant and frankly unhelpful excerpts from Hannah More's *Stories for the Young* (from like the 1800s or something, *definitely* out of copyright, unless the famously terrible Hannah More has been secretly mummified by nefarious Egyptians and prophesied to return before the Long Boring Day of the Egg Collectors — unlikely, given the protection we are afforded by the lizard-king Illuminati in exchange for our freedom and sense of decorum in most but not all public swimming pools), and a pointless but actually rather terrifying and worthwhile excerpt from the gloriously outdated and fascistic book "written so as to give enlightenment to those entering into wedlock so their married life will be one of happiness and pleasure," *Sex Advice to Women* (1917 by R. B. Armitage, M.D.)

This book is non-refundable, in a general, Confucian, rather pessimistic sense. Time, yours and mine, is its own transaction. We have placed the Gold Standard of Ages into the Great Shredder of Nonexistence by mistaking what is worthwhile for what is consumable, and all years are just empty debt now. That is the meaning of "time is money" in certain circles.

A SPLINTER IN YOUR YOUTH

(This story exhibits an accurate picture of that part of the country where the author then resided; and where, by her benevolent zeal, a great reformation was effected among the poor inhabitants of at least twenty parishes, within a circle of thirty miles.)

In a moment he will lose and reinterpret for years, he is jolted, thrown or yanked or shredded into existence. The heaving of his desperate mother stops. What they call sensations overwhelm him. The mess of colors, sounds, grossnesses globular and steaming. They watch him relieved from the bed, professional from the monitors, terrifying from the door where his father enters to see the holy Jesus is that my son.

The family dog destroys a toy. The uncle, who is not an uncle but his father's friend but simplified into an uncle, buys him a more expensive toy.

What he would like for Christmas is the thing he receives, and Christmas turns very dull. Snow for the first time in five years, a slight grazing of condensation you can wipe off the windows while the house is quiet except for the music your father plays and your mother also seems to like jazz.

He has an ear infection, but it goes, and the family dog.

School is many years of insufficient schooling. Life teaches too. According to his uncle. Who runs his own business and speaks differently to each parent.

Could pay more attention during team projects, could contribute more to class discussions, otherwise very polite and well-behaved.

Disciplinary action even though it wasn't even his fault but you can't just treat us both the same when he was the one who hit me first. It's not fair. His parents agree. His mother says it's ridiculous. His father, who has turned to mumbling for most of his conversation, doesn't mumble when he looks at his son's bruise and carefully alerts him to the reality of school bullies — they will always be there. Maybe we should no no let him fend for himself a little we can't just toughen him up like that yes I know but let's wait and not be hysterical. On the other hand he does get a present he wasn't expecting. To cheer him up. He waits before opening it, thoughtful.

The drug discussion is very brief. He doesn't need to be told, he's not doing drugs anyway, trust him. They do. He ends up smoking a single joint in a church graveyard about an hour before school begins. The school day unwinds like tightening coil around the neck of.

Incidentally, the bully has changed schools, which means no more moments of enforced discipline. His grades drop by one percent and the miracle is the weird consistency.

Whatever that was, it was basically sex.

He witnesses his father cooking a steak with: Himalayan salt, chopped onion, just the tiniest, tiniest bit of olive oil until we can get those pans that don't stick and then we can get rid of oil for these kinds of things. The secret to a good steak is don't ever settle for well-done. A steak well-done is a steak poorly done. A good well-done steak is rare. A rare steak is common but a common mistake is not leaving the steak stay rare enough. Further puns. A good rare steak is rarer than gold. Your grandfather used to have gold flakes dropped into his beer on his birthday, and the only thing he wanted was for his friends to chip in to buy the gold flakes and he'd drink that single pint of beer and for the rest of the year he drank nothing only water. You would have liked your grandfather, he was good. I think I cooked this side too much. Flip over like this, let it flip over with the momentum of the pan like… damn it. And that is why your mother does the cooking. And that is why we should call her and maybe you can ask her in your sweetest voice if she could come home on Friday instead of Saturday. I know you're not a child but you're her child. If I use my sweetest voice, well. I'll just be a silly person.

He finds an ember of passion for religion. It burns out and nothing caught fire. Pornography is disgusting. He wakes up filmy with the sweat of guilt. For three months he accidentally ambles toward the same brilliant observation: he wasn't crushed by guilt before the ember of passion for religion. Everything has burned without notice.

Indignation politics time blurs a new war a car accident everyone survives but what a shock. From his hospital bed he sees a nurse spit into a cup.

What bad luck but at least he can say he's had pneumonia now. Someone he meets at a party hilariously calls everyone's attention to how carefully this guy says things like how carefully he pronounces each syllable, ha.

His parents are still married?

For exactly one year he transforms into a woman. Nobody notices because he hasn't told anyone. She takes advantage of the secrecy and observes. She takes advantage of herself. She takes advantage of her blessings. She takes advantage of her talents, which include the following. She takes advantage of a wonderful opportunity. She is not, really, anything. He takes advantage of himself. He takes advantage of being a woman. He takes advantage of his blessings.

His marriage is predicted by the friend of a local drunkard. Perhaps.

Too late to begin keeping notes.

THAT LOMBARDI THING

(An allegory showing how robbers without can never get into a house unless there are traitors within.)

Look, you want the world to conform to your vision, you have to sever some limbs to get there. I'm not a sociopath. I know how this stuff works. Man, I've been doing this for longer than you think. I'm older than you think. You see wrinkles on my face and you assume I'm old, but the truth is I'm older than the wrinkles tell you. And I'm wiser than people give me credit for. Listen to me — you want change, you have to break some bones and screw people over. That's how it works. That's it. I've distilled my wisdom and that's what you get.

Me, I work five hours a day. More than that, and I collapse. I tell you, I'm old, but I'm not just old, I'm a lazy fucker too. My lifestyle, I can't change it anymore. For decades now I've been helping guys like you find influence, or power, or whatever you want to call it. Five hours a day, five days a week, I'm in this shitty basement making kids like you into rock stars, terrorists, whatever. Then I sit back and I snort myself some powder or other and I forget all about you. No offense. I just don't care anymore.

So your girlfriend left you and you want to get her back? Or you're looking for a bunch of punks to boss around for a few months, be a gang leader sort of thing? I can get you that. I can get you anything you want. It's going to cost you, but you'll see that, in the end, it'll have been worth it. But let me tell you what I don't do. One: I am not — I repeat, I'm not — leaving this basement. Whatever materials I need to make your dream come true, it's up to you to get it for me. I live in this house and I will die in this house, and too many motherfuckers are trying to kill me already. I won't risk leaving the house. Hell, I almost never

4

leave the God damned basement. So that's rule number one. Number two is, you pay me first, and you pay me in full, and there are no refunds. I am a professional. I don't fuck up. If you fuck up, that's your damned problem, and I don't care. So if you ask me, for example, to help you stage a coup on some little island in the Pacific, I will help you plan the thing. But if it goes wrong, it's not my fault. You fucked up.

Yeah, I know you're in a hurry. You're in hurry because you're a kid. Chill the hell out. I don't know what you're after and right now that doesn't matter. I want to lay the rules down before we talk business, okay? Okay? Okay. So, rule number three. It is a bad, bad idea to fuck around with language. I know it's all the rage right now, but you don't want to do it. Trust me. I get some intellectual type guy come in here every few weeks, always a different one, and he's all about the relationship between language and reality. Always the same story. Guy wants me to help him overcome the barrier between the linguistically structured universe and the universe as it really is. Well, I am telling you now. You don't want to mess with that stuff. You won't like what you find. See, I can tell from the sulky face you're making that you're one of those intellectual types. You probably heard about the Lombardi thing, and you want to know how you can replicate that. Jesus. Sit down, all right? Let me explain something to you.

The Lombardi thing was a fucking disaster. You don't know what happened, no matter how correct you think your information is. Lombardi was my client, and I know what happened. You want to know? You curious? Okay. I'll tell you. But you'll be disappointed. I'm told people think the Lombardi experiment worked. It didn't. People think Lombardi has crossed the divide between language and the real. He hasn't, or not in the way you think. No sir. There isn't a ferry between the two realms. You know that, right? It's not like I can give you a pill that you take whenever you want to escape the clutches of language.

Lombardi comes to me one day, before I know anything about him, and asks me if I can help hack into his brain. That's how the guy puts it, too — hack into his brain. He's dead serious, of course. He doesn't want me to operate on his head. That's outside my expertise. No, he wants a shortcut. Wants me to help him with this project he's working on. Asks me, "You know anything about Freudhacking?" And me, "What the fuck is Freudhacking? I know Freud. I know hacking. What the fuck is Freudhacking?" And him, "Freudhacking is when you reverse the positions of your conscious and unconscious minds. Like, you flip a switch and the lights go on and off, the same way like that, you bring your unconscious to the foreground and it becomes your conscious, and vice-versa." Well that sounds like horseshit to me, and I tell him, and he's all, "Nah, it works. I know it works. I just don't know how to do it, and the guy who told me about it, he's in jail for dealing." So okay. I make a living doing all sorts of crazy stuff. That's what you pay me for, fine. So what am I meant to do? Read up on this Freudhacking crap? Course, Lombardi just expects me to hand him the answer on a fucking silver platter, and that doesn't happen, ever. I'm here to facilitate, not to work out the mysteries of life while you're jerking off in the waiting room.

Now, this Lombardi character, he's rich. I mean good family. Shady family, I hear, but rich family. And I like making money. Everyone does. And this Lombardi offers me an outrageous sum, we're taking six digits and not just a couple million either. It's more money than I make in six months. You're thinking, why doesn't this idiot just retire, if he's making so much? Well, that's none of your business, and anyway, I like my job. Keeps the demons away. So I start doing some research. Freud, he was a freak, but he was a freaking genius. I mean serious brains on that guy. But the more I read, the more I think this Lombardi is misreading Freud, if he's reading him at all. I've got to work out all these little important details: is the unconscious a structurally necessary part of the mind? Is it there from the start? Is it something you can get rid of? What's in the fucking unconscious, you know? Fantasies about your mother? But the more I'm reading, the more I'm impressed. Freud revises his theories all the time. Whatever works, he keeps. Whatever doesn't, he trashes. Like a good little scientist, and I'm not used to hearing him being called a scientist.

In the end I realize that Freudhacking doesn't have that much to do with Freud at all. They call it Freudhacking because it sounds cool, and because it involves the unconscious and all that shit, but the Freudhacker's conception of the unconscious isn't really Freudian. So I drop my Freud reading and I go through as much underground literature as I can find about the idea of Freudhacking. The bottom line is, Freudhackers think you can bring all the sensory input, all the stuff you aren't aware of when you're walking down the street but your body is still registering, and all the stuff you have in your memory but aren't thinking about at this very moment, to the front of your consciousness, and as a result all the stuff you've been thinking about gets pushed back. You're nodding your head, so I guess you've heard about this. Well, forget it. Freudhacking is no game. The reason this Lombardi wanted to do it was, well, he had artistic motivations. He wanted to let everything he wasn't directly conscious of to permeate his awareness, so that he could try writing a book under that condition. Basically, he's looking for psychoanalytical opium. Fine, I get it. Guy doesn't feel inspired, or thinks everything's already been done — except this one thing, this idea of writing from the unconscious directly, letting all the sensations pour onto the page. Cool enough, as an idea. But the question on my mind is, is it worth the risk?

For one thing, Freudhacking is difficult even on a lucky day. Think about it. You're bringing everything that's incommunicable to light. You're leaving behind the things you can express with words, and opening the floodgates for a whole flood of intensely personal shit, all the things that give you substance as a human being — and all that just to write a damned book? But Lombardi's the customer and I like my money, so I voice my concerns, he dismisses them, and I leave it at that. Far as I'm concerned, my hands are clean.

Now, it's not that I don't want to bore you with details, because details are my specialty — but I'm not going to tell you how Freudhacking works in any great detail. Truth is, I don't know you, and I think if I tell you how to do it, you'll try it out yourself, unsupervised. And that's a bad idea. But you know the basics. You're placed into the nearest state of death before death — in other words, you're placed into a coma. Not quite brain-dead but definitely not conscious in any way whatsoever. This has to be done carefully, of course, and since the practice is, uh, about as illegal as anything else I do, I'd advise against trying even that. But why would you want to, I guess...

Next, I bring you back to life, metaphorically talking. That involves all kinds of medical shit I'm not comfortable with, which is another reason why I don't like doing this. You know what? I'm telling you too much already. The point is, I do certain things while you're knocked out and when I bring you back to consciousness, if you want to call it consciousness, you're completely loopy. You freak out for about a week, a whole week of freaking out and screaming and trying to deal with all the shit you've been burying deep inside you all these years. Everyone's got demons. Problem is, yours are out of the box now. You spend days screaming insults at your dad while you jerk off thinking about your cousin, and so forth. Nasty things happen to you. They call this transference, but it's not a Freudian term, the way they use it. It just means you're transferring all your internal bullshit into the outside world. Your desires are out in the open, and the freaky thing is, you can verbalize them — you can say out loud, to whoever will listen, that you're harboring homo fantasies or whatever. It's all been pulled out of you. You know how once you admit something out loud, it doesn't bother you that much, it loses its edge? Yep. After you've calmed down, which, as I say, takes about a week on average, then you start to live a normal life again, except you're able to make peace with your darkness. Sounds constructive, maybe, right? Well, it isn't. Because, as all the Freudhackers will tell you, once your darkness is on the outside, you start forming a new darkness inside you. You need that unconscious, kid. It will never go away, and in fact it's only going to fill you up with even more bullshit than before.

Now. I read all of this in the Freudhacking literature, and I tell Lombardi what I've found. And his answer, straight away, as though he'd been expecting me to say that stuff all along, is: "If the problem is that, through verbalization of my desires, the unconscious loses its power, maybe I need to find a way to remove language from the equation altogether, right?" And me, "How are you fixing to write a book without language?" And him, "I don't care about the book anymore. I want to escape the world of language. If Freudhacking won't help me, then we have to find something else." And I ask him, "What's language ever done to you that you hate it so much?" And here I am, prepared to hear all his pretentious philosophical shit, but instead he says, "Words hurt. Words limit the way we see the world. I don't want to be able to tell the difference between a table and a chair. I don't want to have the ability to separate one face from another. I want to experience the world as it is when you're a baby, when nobody's placed you in linguistic chains. I have nothing to live for, but I do have this desire. This desperate longing for a life without words."

Well, I was moved. Here was this unhappy fella without good looks to keep him busy. And I was able to help him, right? It's what I do. So we started working together, trying to figure out how to do this removal-of-language thing. It's not easy. The Freudhacking literature had very little to say about this at that point. Back then, before the Lombardi case was famous, it was all about dealing with your demons by dragging your unconscious desires out, etcetera. Now we were pioneers. I'll spare you the details, again, for your own God damned protection. But what we decided to try was to follow the advice of one Freudhacker, this guy called Schreiber, who claimed to have been able to transgress the limits of language during an experiment he conducted on himself, with the help of his girlfriend. So what happened was this Schreiber subjects himself to a real rough treatment. I mean, we're talking dangerous here. He gets his girlfriend to knock him out using a drug — no, I'm not telling you which drug, don't be a moron. Knocks him out cold, leaves him in a coma. Imagine seeing your lover in a coma. Christ almighty. Anyway, for the next month — takes him a month to get out of that coma — his girlfriend takes excellent care of her comatose boyfriend, keeps a constant eye on him, cleans his shit, and so on, but she doesn't say a word to him. Instead, there's a recording, a single word, playing into his ears through headphones, all the time. All the time that he's in a coma, his ears are being filled with a looped recording of his girlfriend saying "lallum." Fucking lallum. It doesn't mean anything, and that's the point. It could've been any word, but it has to be a word that means nothing to the listener. Now — thirty days of this. The point of the experiment, I should add, wasn't to sever ties with language or whatever. It was to see if you could actually hear things when you were in a coma. If, when he woke up, he remembered the word lallum, then he'd know it was possible. That was it — these Freudhackers will do anything in the name of research. They're the real scientists, these underground freaks.

Anyway, Schreiber wakes up after about a month and he can't talk. He can't say a word except... lallum. For weeks he's incapable of saying anything other than lallum, and it doesn't mean anything to him. He'll just mumble it to himself sometimes. Otherwise he's sitting around staring at things for hours and hours. Hears her speak but doesn't seem to understand what she's saying. Doesn't ask for anything. Shits right where he's sitting. When he's hungry he walks around and puts things in his mouth. Like a big baby. And then one day... he snaps right out of it. He's back to talking like an adult. And he describes those weeks as the most peaceful, the most beautiful moments of his life. He didn't feel time pass him by. Everything was unbelievably interesting. All those sensations. And you ask him why he sometimes said lallum, and, well, he doesn't know. Just hasn't got a clue.

So Lombardi wants to try that, too. Dangerous, right? But he wants to try it and he's willing to buy his way there, so we do it. Fucking mistake. At first it all goes fine. I drug him, he slips into the darkness, and I keep earphones in his ears. The word, this time, is "torua." I made it up. Didn't mean anything to me, or to him. But he stays in that coma for a long, long time. The weeks go by and I'm paying someone to watch over him while I start taking on other cases, because the fucker just doesn't leave his comatose state. I just assume Lombardi is good as dead, but I'm not pulling the plug or anything. So I wait. I wait and months pass. The nurse quits and I take on another one. And he quits too. So I find a third one, and this one is a major dyke, but she's good. She sits by Lombardi's side reading a book, and never complains. Takes good care of him. But one day she comes up and interrupts me to say Lombardi's gone. Gone how? He's brain-dead. He's breathing but his brain is fried. So I sigh, and I go downstairs and I have a look and sure enough, after messing around with the machines, I know the nurse is right. Lombardi is brain-dead. He's officially a goner, but technically he's still alive. And then the weirdest, freakiest thing in my life happens — he starts to speak. His eyes open but he doesn't look at anything in particular, and he starts saying random things. "Vessel vassal vascular" and "ping pong pang" and other combinations of words that don't make any sense. I sit there staring at him for a good hour, wondering what's happening. Then I tell the nurse to call me if anything new happens, and I go back upstairs.

Two weeks of this. Two weeks of incoherent rambling from Lombardi. He's not aware of anything. He's like a robot that says random words. And the nurse, she's getting weirded out by all this. I understand her, too. Sitting alone with a brain-fried dude who looks around and spouts nonsense strings of words, well, it freaks me out too. But I tell her I'll double her pay if she stays. I can afford it, since I made Lombardi pay up front. So she stays. Another two weeks pass. Then another two. And then, one night, Lombardi just kicks the bucket. Dead — just like that. Heart stops beating, mouth stops moving, and the nurse begins to cry. She was starting to consider him her friend or something. Well, I pay her an extra nice sum and tell her that if anyone asks about this, the story is that Lombardi was happy with the experiment and is now living in Italy or some place like that. Under no circumstances must she disclose the truth. She agrees, and off she goes, and now you know where those rumors began, the rumors about the Lombardi thing being a success.

Some success. As far as I understand it, when his brain got fried, Lombardi died, but for some reason the language inside him lived on. Make of that what you will. Talking to you makes me realize just how old I really am. Maybe I should retire. I'm rich enough. I've seen enough. I've done my part in the Freudhacking world — and like I said, you have to break some bones if you want to make progress. Maybe someday I'll write all this up for the Freudhackers to look over. But that's not my scene. Now get out of here, kid. I need to be alone.

ACTS

(The right way of rejoicing at Xmas, showing the reasons we have for joy at the event of our Savior's birth.)

A eunuch born of dark hot distant Ethiopia returning from Jerusalem reading Isaiah, understanding nothing, glancing at the sand with tired red eyes wondering at the words, meaningless thing-like oppressive words: desert all around; invisible torrents of warmth soaking through every cranny on his body forcing eunuch skin to glisten. A man of power, status & God who watches planning, God with his son again but childless guiding another youth across the desert toward the chariot where the eunuch sits. This youth is Philip. Curls rolling from his shoulders, brown-green eyes, shoulders as broad as any mother could have wished. Philip aglow with the beauty of his message & the bravery of his mission, asking the eunuch from Ethiopia: "What book is that between your hands? & can you grasp it? & has it sense?" "I feel a fool for trying," says the eunuch, & Philip reads the words aloud: "He was like a lamb to the slaughter, & like a lamb dumb before his shearer — & from this," Philip whispering, "we may start & plunge into your own infinity" & Philip preaches to him Jesus, child of God & man, whose life & death & life will be our debt & our ascent. They sit together on the chariot riding to Ethiopia, the eunuch listening & questioning & doubting & believing, Philip answering, insisting nothing, because truth is not in teachings but in the death of God, his proof, his quiet simple agony. The eunuch struggling not to believe; cursing the Word, its fragile enunciation, the sound of it spoken from the lips of the beauty beside him. It matters nothing what the Word is; only say it & remember & treat it with respect — every word forming worlds is good & needed & any word could end the chain of meaning — so may the stream of words from Philip's mouth ring true beyond the factuality of truth, & let there be no need to understand the secret syntax of what has being said. It simply needs the saying the irrational adoration flowering over us stupidly & totally & always. The Word is never One, the Word is the space for combinations of words, the space for declarations of love, affirmations of faith, legislations for holocausts, questions of value, directions for pilgrimage, denials of truths — the Word encircling the eunuch, giving off a different warmth, a pleasant, cooling life in death, & Jesus — no longer listening to Philip's words & guiding them into our bodies — has entered the darkest regions of the eunuch's stupid heart & thickened the ventricles, thickened the blood, thickened the skin around the muscles, strengthened the bones, not as repayment but acknowledgement: of the primacy of life before death, life before the Everlasting, the blessing of finitude & boundedness in time, the all-important stumbling that cripples or forces to run, depending — the words from Philip's lips like singing & language irrelevant, the intonations more melody than body & when they come to water on the ground, a miracle already in this desert, the eunuch points & howls from joy: "Can I not be baptized now? I believe, but am not forced, because I have no proof, because I have a heart & mind & I can walk & I can speak, & for this I owe gratitude to God, who gave me ears, & to you, who taught me to listen, & to Jesus, who gave me things to hear. I have no need of faith, & have proof of spirit, & even without proof I have life & lifeless I have death, & my gratitude will not expire, & if it is to Jesus I must speak & send my thanks & praises & to his father & to the space his father occupies, then I wish to be baptized today & for good, to begin continually…" Philip baptizing the eunuch in the water, & the Lord, mute idiot boundless good & true, lowering an unseen hand to whisk away the young apostle, the eunuch rejoicing & kneeling, water dripping from his temples, thanking the sand & thanking the sky & thanking all, the brute matter of thingness, the words, the Word, its author & its speaker & looking upward at his friend he finds himself alone. Philip is nowhere.

EX LIBRIS

(Being the seventh sign that Satan is Lord, but only when the Lord lies sleeping)

This will be a brief tale, because the affair was brief. I refuse to be too literary about it. The fact is that I am always sabotaging my chances at happiness, and now that all of this cute and romantic mediocrity is past, I can tell myself I am free, if nothing else.

There was a young woman I managed to fall for, a blonde, if that matters, but not stupid.

She had a good enough collection of books, including some very strange, rusty paperbacks of the Shakespeare canon. I don't know why that should have bothered me so much, but the rustiness appalled me. It was the first hint that I was losing the struggle against whatever was in me. "Books shouldn't be rusty."

"I found these in a metal crate when my father died," she said. "It's not like the paper's rusty through some kind of magic."

It didn't matter at the time. We moved in together. She wanted to keep her books with mine. She said it was only natural to keep books together.

"But my books are my books."

"They'll still be your books."

To be clear: I did love her. I wanted to make her happy, or at least to see her smile because of me once or twice a day. It was all kind of cute and mostly meaningless, the way love is when it's new and kicking in the womb. So we put the books together. Soon we had a nice little library.

Her favorite novels were *Wuthering Heights*, which is fair, and The Gospel of John. "That is not a novel," I informed her.

"Yes, it is. It's not non-fiction."

"It's from the New Testament. It's not a novel."

"Well, it is."

"It predates 'the Novel' by millennia."

"If I don't read it as a novel, I can't read it at all. So I read it as a philosophical novel, and then I enjoy it a good deal."

"So St John was like Sartre to you."

"No, more like Cervantes."

Again: I loved her, and didn't want to upset her. So I said nothing else, and had an enormous and perhaps hysterical rant running in my head for the rest of the afternoon.

It was a beautiful, ceremonial thing. We made love twice a day at least; the fluids and the sounds were love, the sweating and the panting were love, everything was love in the fullest and darkest, most rebellious sense. When she broke into tears over trivial things, the way I had sworn no woman I could love would ever do, I comforted her. I held her hand. I made her laugh occasionally, something I am proud of still. I was never very good at making others laugh.

The library bothered me, though. I didn't want our books together. Perhaps, probably, I felt superior to her. She called the Book of John a novel. She had never managed to read Moby-Dick, because she thought it was meant for men and men only. Her prejudices ran as deep as mine. I couldn't read Jane Austen because of whatever. She couldn't read Cortázar because of whatever else. We disagreed on all the things that should have brought us intellectual pleasure. I woke up one morning with the feeling, a vague and indeterminate awareness, that I had dreamed for hours of raping her while lecturing her on all the novels she should read. It was a matter of pride, narcissism, and a burgeoning lust for something she could not give me.

Because I had fallen in love, my sense of who I was had widened and narrowed at the same time. When she was cheerful, I was irritated. When she wasn't, I spent my energy trying to make her feel better again. By the time I knew how to predict her mood swings, I knew I loved her more profoundly than I had ever loved anyone, because she didn't quite bore me even after a few months.

But the books. How to accept seeing my books next to hers, or between hers, or on top of hers, or open and lying next to hers, or in between her pretty little hands? What if she noticed my inscriptions, my underlinings, and began to understand what had shaped me, the things I had found worthy of my time, the aphorisms worth circling in case someday their wisdom might come in handy? What if she somehow managed to piece me together simply by knowing what I'd read, what I'd noted in the margins as the observations came to me, what pages I'd torn out of otherwise impressive novels because the author had just this once managed to fuck up his prose or because my greedy grubby little hands had smeared the pages so badly that the words became illegible and God forbid anyone see the stains and the smudges and the scribbles when all of this was mine now, this was my text, this was my novel and the original author was dead and only I could truly know what had happened to those pages I had ripped out and shredded up to keep my wisdom a secret? She was in that unenviable but fascinating place, she could see through my eyes and read my mind simply by figuring out why certain words were crossed out, why the margins contained or didn't contain references to other books (this made me think of that, Faulkner is clearly not aware that this did not actually happen in the French trenches, where the hell did Sancho Panza's mule come back from — I thought it had been stolen) so fuck her, she had no right and probably no inclination but more impor-tantly no right to be going through my intellectual history, there for her to rifle through and scrutinize and somehow get me and what I was about, what sense I had made of the world, what mattered to me beyond her.

I said this would be a brief tale. Let me end, then, by explaining why I had to end things with her. Love is opening up, removing stitches prematurely, letting the wound tremble in the sunlight. I didn't want to open up quite as much as the sharing of our books demanded. But there was more than my idea of myself at stake. One day, I found her reading the book of recipes that I'd taken from my grandmother's house, the book with pictures of cakes and millefeuilles and pies, my grandmother's kitchen-life and my only memory of her — and I never much cared for anyone in my family, so this is doubly strange — and I screamed. It all got too much, maybe. Now she could see not just my trajectory, but my grandmother's. Now she had access to my thoughts and those to whom I owed my life. She knew which recipes my grandmother had circled with a huge marker because they'd been such a success. She could interpret it all, could guess which cakes I had eaten as a child, could see the crumbs that had slipped into the abyss between each couple of pages, could even, if she wanted, put the crumbs to her mouth and taste the past.

So I almost, but not quite, but almost, grabbed the nearest book, a conveniently thick hardback, probably Melville, probably Moby-Dick, and lifted it way up over my head before bringing it back down onto her skull with a crack and a spurt of blood that sprayed against my face and blinded me for a few red seconds. I almost bashed her with my copy of Moby-Dick until her nose had sunk into her face so deeply that the roof of her mouth had been torn in the process. I almost yanked out every page of Ishmael's classic narrative and force-fed them to her. I almost sat down the floor next to her blood-gushing convulsing body and explained to her, in the most controlled voice I could muster, why the fuck she should stop calling the Book of John a novel. It's not a novel. I love you, and I respect you, but you really sound like an idiot when you try to sound clever like that. It's not a novel. It's part of the New Testament. It's probably the most beautiful Gospel. It calls into question a lot of the assumptions you might make while reading the other three. Calling it a novel doesn't make you sound like you know what you're talking about. It just betrays a profound ignorance of literary history. And to be honest, I don't really believe you when you say it's one of your favorites. I don't get the impression you mean it. Maybe you do. But if you're just saying it to sound sophisticated, you don't need to try and impress me. I like who you are, and I don't care if your favorite novel is *Wuthering Heights*. Why should I care? I'm happy with you. We don't have to play intellectual games. Let's just, oh, come here. I love you and you don't need to cry about this. Emily Bronte is a perfectly good choice. Let's not get upset about this.

LETTER

(The parable of the laborers in the vineyard at Corinth)

Dear —,

You are holding in your veiny little hands the absolute truth, the final answer you've been searching for. You can probably tell by my handwriting who I am. I have the worst handwriting you have ever seen; you told me so. But if you can't, I will sign my name at the bottom. Have a look, if you haven't already.

I should make two things clear before I reveal all of this to you. Firstly, I am not insane. Others will chalk it up to my "history" of mental illness. You will not, because you will have read this letter and you will be quite aware that I have not "gone mad" — as everyone you show this to will want to put it. Secondly, you are not to blame for any of this, not quite. You are a nice lady. I enjoyed your lessons. There was no reason for me to do what I did, and the sooner you accept that, the sooner you believe that, the better. No doubt I should not be dishing out advice to the woman whose son I murdered. Take it with a pinch of salt, but trust that I am earnest.

A final caveat. If you choose to read this letter in its entirety, you will feel nauseated. I am going to describe absolutely everything about your son's murder — everything that can be described — but I won't give you any reasons. There are no reasons. This will be the most difficult thing for you to deal with, because, as Timothy himself put it so many times, nothing is more terrifying than sudden senselessness. I believe he was inspired by the work of Joseph Conrad — I think, in fact, that your husband (God rest his soul, of course) was the one who gave Timothy a copy of The Secret Agent, which deals with just this kind of mentality. Things have come a long way since Conrad's day — it is both easier and more difficult to track down

21

terrorists; airplanes are everywhere; there have been worldwide wars — but occasionally one catches a glimpse of the dark nature of progress: you can anesthetize all you want, but you cannot stop the void from engulfing things. Your son is dead.

I will not ramble. If my tone displeases you, as it no doubt does, you will want to put this letter down every few lines as you read. So here is a summary for you. Read it, then call your doctor and the police, and when you get the chance again, read the rest of this letter. I killed your son two days ago, in a hut, out in the woods, with a rock. I simply picked up a heavy rock and struck him on the head with it. The body is not mutilated, but it is rotting away. Attached is a map to help you find whatever remains of him, which isn't much. That is the short version.

The long version goes as follows. When you used to give me lessons in Latin, you were a wonderful tutor. My parents were delighted with my progress, and I only told them nice things about you. There are no complaints on my end — superb pedagogy. Without your help I would never have been invited to study where I did, and for that I have to thank you. You were patient, friendly, careful. You made me not only read Latin, but also speak it — and write it. I have dear memories of sitting at that tiny table where you used to make me work, a table that I now realize was meant for playing Bridge. You are a Bridge player. This suits the memory I have of you perfectly.

While my classmates found Latin a dreary chore, I excelled at it. Of course I did. You were there for me. Thanks to you I was one of those teenagers pretending to live in the wrong era, writing letters instead of sending emails, reading classical texts instead of fantasy novels, Hazlitt not Hitchens, placing clever Latin phrases in my notes for those who were "in" on this kind of thing. And you saw this in me — and encouraged it. I was so starved for attention that I even tried to impress you, a harmless, sad lady whose recognition ought to have meant nothing to me. Still I strove for attention and you, in your erudition and kindness, fostered that spirit in me. When I was sent off as an undergraduate to a weird and wider world, I missed having your gaze on me. I suppose I felt misunderstood all over again. You had given me confidence, and I had lapped up your praise — worthless, patronizing flattery, yes, but fabas indulcet fames. It was all I could get.

None of this is really relevant, but it might inform your reading of the juicy bit. I am trying to show that I have nothing against you specifically. I owe a great deal to you, and I acknowledge it. So why did I kill your son? Remember: you will not have an answer to this. He is dead. You have not heard from him since he disappeared, and you have been thinking the worst. Deep down, you surely have worried that something terrible happened to him. And you are right about that. I hit him on the skull with a pointy rock. There was a crack. There was blood, and grunting, and twitching — then nothing.

The hut where Timothy's body will soon be discovered is nothing majestic, not a dignified place to die. It is a hut that used to belong to a lumberjack of sorts. The type of quiet, heavy-thinking, heavy-drinking man we are all familiar with from novels. I suppose you could describe him as a real-life Mellors, from that Lawrence book you defended so vigorously when the school forbade Timothy from writing about it in an essay. You have always had an open mind about literature. I know Tim was thankful for that, at least. You came to the fore, cast shame on the reactionary fools running our fine school. We were all surprised. "Nobody should stop a young man from reading a classic work of literature," you said, "no matter how scandalized people may have claimed to be by it half a century ago." Indeed. You looked out for our best interests. Half the school had a copy of Lady Chatterley's Lover by the time the fiasco was over. This is how it always goes. But back to the Mellors-like ogre who used to live in the hut. He died about five years ago, I suppose. I could be wrong. He died and left behind some broken bottles, rags, a mattress now covered in moss. You'll see all of this when you go out to find the mess.

Confession. At first I considered playing games with you: not just the cruel games I am playing with you now in this quite innocent letter, but real catch-me-if-you-can games in a spirit so disgusting, so relentlessly cynical that you'd probably have had a heart attack by the second minute. I wanted to send you pictures of Timothy's corpse, with little clues. Ways for you to find your beloved son. I wanted to call you in the middle of the night and whisper the things I had done to him. None of this, I'm happy to say, seemed very realistic. It could be done, but other people had done it already. I will not give you a list of killers who played games with their victims; that would be a waste of time. The point is that I hit Timothy with a rock and that is it. That's all. After this letter you will never hear from me again. This is a promise and an admission of guilt at the same time.

Nevertheless I have to manipulate you a little bit, because if I don't this letter will lose its impact. I would like to tell you about Timothy, to give you a friend's impression to complement your parental ideas about who your son was. You saw him as an intelligent, innocent, good-looking boy. The truth, I'm thrilled to say, is that he really was all of these things. He was intelligent, far more intelligent than most gave him credit for. He was innocent, yes — innocent enough to have found it necessary to respect all your wishes. When he wanted to do something dangerous — say, when he wanted to learn to drive — you would not let him. He was twenty-one and you still asked him not to drive. He often lamented these little things and resented you for them. For all your bravado about freedom of expression, reading "dangerous" novels, and so on, you were an overbearing and overprotective mother to him. And because he was good looking, you also feared the loose girls in our neighborhood for a while. You wanted nothing to take him away from you.

Which always ends badly. In Tim's case, having you as a

mother made him bitter. He didn't realize it; why should he? You treated him like a little prince, and being sheltered was no reason to be bitter. But he was — he was a bitter, unhappy kid. You gave his classmates Latin lessons while he played with his toys in his room. Some of us called him the Roman. He spoke fluent Latin and wore outmoded clothes. It was a strange thing to do, teaching him to speak some kind of Latin as well as he spoke English. It wasn't strange to him, of course. He was comfortable with the situation. Dulcis domus.

That is one of the problems of living with others — that sinking into normality, or maybe I should call it settling, how we feel comfortable with the way we are treated no matter how unfairly that may be, simply because we've come to know our place. If I learned any grand, important lesson from studying Petronius, Pindar, all the way to Montaigne — I am listing names almost at random — it is that the task of fitting in does not grow less important with time. Not on the historical, human scale. The urge to belong somewhere doesn't lessen; it can be buffered by the illusion that we have finally found out where we should be, but that is a small comfort. And Timothy, your son, acted the way you thought your son Timothy should act. He didn't forge himself a new way of life until he moved out, until he and I became friends. I'm sorry — I considered your baby a true friend, and I still killed him, and it was in vain. I still don't know where I belong; it didn't help. But I did learn something from this. I know, now, that I can still feel love, passion, regrets, amusement, boredom, hope, whatever, I can still feel these things even after killing my friend. The faculties, the emotions have not changed. It seems there really is something fundamental about me, something that doesn't change through my actions. I don't know what it is, but perhaps I'll find out when all of this passes over.

You thought Timothy was a good-natured guy, and he was. He was absurdly good-natured. He was generous, hard-working, occasionally funny, always friendly. I am bringing this up because I want you to have these things in mind when I describe how the rock pierced his skull — effortlessly, like a needle piercing a balloon, only without the pop. In fact the only sound was his gurgling, the guh-guh-glub in his throat as he fell to the floor and began to overflow with blood, beautiful wine-dark blood rushing out like waves from the wound. It wasn't pleasant for me, either. Still, I left him there to die and went for a nice walk in the woods. As I walked under the shades of trees I couldn't name, the sun nearly blinding me whenever it could break through the branches and the leaves, I didn't think of Timothy. I didn't think of much at all. I was a little numb, but the numbness was only right. There was so much to do in the world.

I have a little more to say. It is about you. I'm running out of time — my lover will soon be waking up; I need to hide this letter — so I will say it outright: you are not to blame for this if you don't wish to be. No doubt you have felt racked with guilt since Tim disappeared, or, more precisely, since he disappeared immediately after that argument you two had. You are exactly right: that argument, the one you're thinking of this very second. It was, I hear, an unpleasant one. The way he told it, I got the feeling you two were set on never speaking to each other again when he vanished. Are things beginning to make sense? It took place in your living room — he was sitting at the Bridge table, and you were seated, glacially, indignantly, a few feet away on the couch I once spilled juice on. (To your credit, you never charged us for that little accident.) You have probably played this scene out in your mind several times over by now. How you lost your composure when he told you. Well, if it helps you make sense of all this, you can tell yourself that that little argument was the reason this happened.

All those Latin lessons have amounted to nothing. I am no better off now for having taken them. I don't think I have gained anything from the books I've read, or the abstractions I've tackled. In the end, I consist of a few past actions and many missed opportunities, and that's what I'll be remembered for. The same is true of Tim. You will, I imagine, remember him as a nice, sinful (oh no!), confused, unfulfilled, handsome, temperate boy, not as the little faggy homosexual queer fudgepacking boy lover that he turned out to be. Having said all this, it's amusing that it was because of the Latin that Tim and I became friends, and even more amusing that the opportunities we didn't miss are the ones that led to everyone's downfall here.

Explanation, in case you're still figuring it out. One day, maybe a year ago — around the time Tim came out of that dark, mothball-stinking closet — I walked with him in the woods, and we found the abandoned hut. We used it to store books, musical instruments, weed, etcetera. Mostly books. We went there to talk about life and the cosmos and women. It was early afternoon the time that I heard him share his views on death (it was early afternoon the time I started thinking I should send him death's way). He had a peculiar, ironic philosophy. The world is pain, he said, but so is it pleasure, and surely separating the afterlife into good and bad is nonsense. Such a vision of the world after this world is silly. Why not, if we are going to parse out the emotions this way, see what comes next as a movement from pain to less pain, or pleasure to less pleasure? Why not imagine a state in which we move from total, tragic, endless suffering to greater and greater relief, not joy? In the first second of your death, you find yourself at the heights of despair; then, little by little and for the rest of eternity, you suffer less and less, never quite reaching pleasure but never going back to the ball of agony that encapsulated you at the start? Continual relief — isn't that better than static bliss? And if you want a Hell, as you surely do, since you think Tim is going there, then picture an orgasm that just gets more and more grating, forever sliding downwards into the Horror, at first a beautiful relief and then inch by inch the realization that you will never feel as good as you do right now — and now you feel worse — and now worse still — ad infinitum. That was Tim's half-jesting alternative to the bore of a God-granted Heaven and a Devil-infested Hell. Theological matters were always on his mind, as you must know; you shoved them in there, after all.

Well! Hearing this while jugging down a bottleful of your late husband's whisky (who else was going to drink it?), struggling, in my own way, with my various Heavens and Hells, I found myself distracted by the apparition of the amatory ghost (which is what Timothy called a rock-hard boner). Now let me be clear that this is where the death of your son is going to be recounted most explicitly. Think of it as a character assassination, not an actual death. What do two lonely, confused, intellectual, horny boys sitting in a hut in the woods have in common? Riddle! What do you think the answer is? Clue: the nerve-wracking, boner-intensifying, uncomfortably happy question we all ask ourselves before we kiss someone for the first time. Is this really happening? Not: Am I gay? (Of course you're gay. Why would you wonder this when you're about to kiss a boy for the first time?) Not: Am I a sinner? (That comes later, when Mother proves displeased.) Not even: What am I doing? (You know exactly what you are doing.) Instead, you wonder if it's all really happening. Are you finally going to kiss the guy you've been pining for? Are you reading his gaze correctly? I have been with women as well, ma'am. I know the feeling is the same, at least in the heat of pre-coital delirium. So this is it? One minute we're talking about Heaven and Hell, secretly imploring the gods to let us get all this chatter out of the way at last and just fuck each other's heads right off — and the next, we're fucking each other's heads right off. Years of friendship and all we really wanted was this! This mouth-to-mouth declaration of submission to the boner, and never mind what Mother will think, never mind the crucifixes or the "social consequences" or how rotted this mattress in this little hut is!

But the crucial bit in all of this, and you will hate yourself for it, or maybe you'll sigh with relief, is that after this first sexual encounter between me and your Tim (well, my Tim), we of course rushed toward saying those final three words that everyone wants to hear and say. It was especially important, given that neither of us had ever been with a man before, and, oh no, it felt right, it felt right for the first time — we were gay. That was it. We were in love, etcetera, and we no longer really cared what Tim's old-fashioned mother might think. You, the weird woman obsessed with letting high school kids read Lady Chatterley's Lover, and also obsessed with the problem of homosexuals — you paradox, you human thing. You were certainly on Tim's mind when he kissed me a few weeks after we first made love and said, in a good, steady, almost confident voice: Te amo. Three glorious words condensed into two glorious words. And in the Latin you taught us.

That's the beautiful thing, or perhaps I should say: that's one of the beautiful things about this past year. There have been setbacks — like your little ugly stupid outburst when he told you last week he "thought" he was gay — but really, I am happy. And although I have murdered many things in this letter, slashed your bigotry at the neck and strangled my chances of ever being on good terms with you again, clubbed your impression of me as a sane and polite guy, sodomized your son, and given you the fabulous vision of a life without your boy (who, I admit, does not know I am writing this letter), I am happy. And so is he.

Tim is about to wake up. You won't be seeing him again. We're off, and he no longer cares, and by now it will be clear to you that you've been sweating quite a bit, and for no real reason. I do not apologize for murdering him in your eyes, but if you're any kind of mother, you'll be relieved first and infuriated later. Amor vincit omnia!

Yours,

—

THE MATURITY OF THE FLY

("You cannot, child," returned Rachel, in a solemn tone; "it is out of your power; you are fated *to marry the grey eyes and light hair.")*

The topic today is the maturity of the fly, which means nothing, but it will let these poor fools say things without being ridiculed. According to one man: "The fly is mature when it stops being a maggot." That is his kind-of scientific perspective, but he knows he's not fooling anyone, and anyway he has more to say. So: "A fly, in other words, reaches its maturity when it discards all maggoty characteristics. By which I mean that a fly can only become an adult — that is, it only turns into a death-driven thing, maybe — when its maggot phase proves unsuitable for its evolving needs."

This is a metaphor, and everyone understands that, apart from the prettiest girl in the room sitting on the only chair that isn't made of wood. They gave her a metal chair. She is uncomfortable. She's been shifting in her seat for a while now. "What needs does a fly have?" she asks.

Oh, they can have fun now. "A fly has many needs. What does a maggot need? Some flesh to roll around in. But eventually the maggot needs more things. Or, perhaps, we could say it... learns to want things." The man, who is attracted to the girl and resents her for it, carries on. "As a maggot, the little soul yearns for nothing. As a fly, it yearns for so much it sprouts wings and does the impossible: it flies. And still its desires — that is the keyword, isn't it — still its desires stretch it in impossible directions. Eventually the fly dies from frustration."

The coordinator of the event, a little Asian man whom everyone has noticed is Asian and somehow that bothers them even though they are all beyond that kind of thing, breaks it up. "Let's not get sidetracked." But nobody listens because, once again, his Asianness is on display. Every academic, black or white, male or female, every academic in the room looks at the Asian coordinator and feels, well, uncomfortable, without knowing exactly why, maybe something about the word — Asian — that means so much and yet says too little about his origins, if the world is really meant to be split between west and east, or north and south, or maybe it's something to do with his sheer humanness, the human skin (slightly yellow, slightly dry) that seems both instantly real and patently false, because it's foreign enough that it's scary but familiar enough that it's scary too. Or something. The worst part is they can't justify it to themselves, and everyone in the room thinks he or she is the only member of the group to harbor that type of secret racism. "You were saying."

"I was saying, I think, that the fly dies from frustration. Isn't that so? Isn't that what everyone who's lucky enough to grow old ends up dying from — frustration? A terrible dissatisfaction with the pleasures we have received."

"I don't think that's true," the pretty girl says.

"You don't, don't you?"

"No, I think we can be satisfied once in a while."

"If you are satisfied once in a while, that leaves a lot of time for being frustrated. But," playing his game again, smirking at his audience, "we are not talking about you, miss, unless you are a fly. The fly is the most tragic creature, because it lives with humans but is hated by them all. Flies are the Jews of the order of insects, and nobody likes them, and nobody can quite say white."

This is a slip. He was going to say "why" but somewhere along the circuit everything got screwed up. So nobody can quite say white. Which, inevitably, but horribly, everyone, black or white, male or female, looks with the greatest subtlety at the Asian coordinator again. That yellow, unwelcome skin. He is the Jew of the academic kingdom. And nobody can quite say white, but there's a rising feeling of contempt in the air. As though the presence of this little man, who has done nothing wrong, whose interests are compatible with those of everyone around, were enough to just, uh, piss you off. Piss you off for no reason. Just because he's around. And maybe it's not his skin color. Nobody here is racist, exactly. There's got to be something else. Something he said once, which upset his listeners, maybe. Or his politics. Maybe you've heard something about his political opinions. He is not this enough, or that enough. He voted for McCain, maybe. He didn't, but, you know, maybe.

"The fly is the martyr, the sufferer, the dog of animals." This is poetic. "Of all the great poets, I believe only Blake ever managed to capture something of the condescension with which we address the Other that is the fly."

Am not I / A fly like thee? / Or art not thou / A man like me? Is that what he's referring to? The Asian coordinator knows he's being watched. God. Something in my teeth, around my mouth? They're noticing that I'm getting a potbelly? They've got nothing to judge me for. It's just a potbelly.

"I want to be clear," the man says, clasping his hands together. "The fly is not just a fly. The fly, in its infinite suffering and frustration, is a symbol. A symbol of, and for, the man who crushes it with a careless hand. The fly, with its stupid and relentless desire, with its wings that give it no real power, no true power, with its grotesque, hairy appearance that you can only see as beautiful when you are close enough for it to disgust you, the fly is a monster we, the people on the planet we call Earth, have created. Flies, which we claim have no purpose and no meaning, are an extension of our narcissism. They are there for us to swat, to kill, our brethren, vicariously, without consequences, without even the Law swooping down and plucking us out of our moral comfort and sending us off to the gallows. If we didn't have flies, whose desires we surely recognize as our own, whose fate is ours, how would we get our kicks from pointless murder? If there were no flies, and nothing to stand in for flies, wouldn't we eventually kill each other out of an insane but constant need for violence?"

There are no flies in the room. It is too cold for flies.

"The more flies we kill, the more we become flies ourselves: tragic and disposable. The day will come when we think we've killed all the flies, and the species will die out. And that is when the maggots in our corpses will develop brains, mouths with tongues, opposable thumbs, and they will finally say to each other with the organs they've taken from us: It is our time now."

The pretty girl objects again. "Wasn't our theme supposed to be the maturity of the fly? What's that got to do with this apocalyptic stuff?"

"Apocalyptic?" The lecturing type shrugs. "It's not apocalyptic."

"Listen," the Asian coordinator says. "We've let this go on for too long." Oh Christ they're all looking at me what the hell are they looking at act calm act unfazed. "We need to move on to the next speaker. Professor, uh, Christopher Hamburg from the University of, uh..." What the hell why are they looking at me like this as if I'd done something wrong they didn't have to attend if they didn't want this is ridiculous stop sweating they'll notice if I keep sweating and maybe that's why they're staring in the first place. "The University of..."

Professor Hamburg stands up. "Thanks for introducing me. I'm going to make my contribution quite short, like the lifespan of the common housefly. Let me preface this by saying that there's no such thing as a common housefly. It's a generic term we use to refer to unwanted winged insects that aren't obviously bees or wasps. Isn't that so?"

Some people nod. Enough to propel the good professor forth.

"Well. My theme is the idea of the common housefly. Let's think about this for a second. We speak of the common housefly with only a vague notion of what it is we're speaking about. We take it for granted, in our daily discourse, that the common housefly is a thing: that a house must have flies, and that a particular type of fly lives in houses. Peculiar — but let's dig deeper. What does it mean for a fly to live in a house? What does it say about us? We, the territorial creatures who shoot strangers sneaking into our house at night, and who swat flies that ought, by the suggestion of their name, be accepted into our living space — what have we got to lose from letting flies live in our homes? This is, of course, a false problem, because, as I've said, and I will insist on this: there is no such thing as a common housefly. No housefly has ever existed, because flies don't live in houses. They live wherever they can. And we don't welcome them into our houses. In a credit crunch, maybe, when there are too many houses sitting unoccupied for someone of my convictions to be comfortable with, you might expect flies to swarm to those unoccupied houses and take up residence. But they don't — because there is no such thing as a common housefly."

Nobody is listening to Professor Hamburg. They consider him stupid, but there's something else. The Asian coordinator, during the professor's talk, has, it seems, lost it. Lost his marbles. Lost his mind. Whatever you want to call it. People can tell. Even the pretty girl can tell, and she's not looking at him. Something about the tiny tremors in the Asian coordinator's body, as though some giant army of maggots had seized his insides, rocking it in all directions. Saying: Our turn. The man, with skin once so uncomfortably yellow and speech patterns so unsettlingly human, is turning into...

"The common housefly is really just what we pin our hopes on. Our dreams. Our failures."

No, he's not turning into anything. He's just nervous. Because we're all looking at him. Ignore and listen to the professor, please. We all came here to hear important thinkers thinking importantly about important things.

"Houseflies are chimerical. Show me a housefly, and I'll show you the source of the universe."

The minutes of this conference will not mention the most tragic aspect of the whole circus. When the Asian coordinator goes home tonight, he will think of his life, think of the maturity of the fly, the speakers, the pretty girl, everything, and he will decide that today was not a good day. He met nobody interesting. He hasn't found a wife. He's not even aware that what so unsettled his colleagues and guests today was his skin, his yellowness. Well. That's beside the point. That was a red herring, as was everything about today. Everything about his entire life so far has been a red herring. He doesn't like organizing conferences. It's thankless. It's boring, pretentious. Nobody listens to anyone else. They're all trying to impress each other with rhetoric and pseudo-Derridean observations about nothing at all. He gained nothing from today. He falls asleep on the couch, and snores. Out of nowhere — literally, out of nowhere, it's winter — a fly starts zipping around. It gets sucked into the void of his mouth. He wakes up choking. He chokes to death.

A DREAM IN GERMAN PROVES UNSATISFYING AS A METAPHOR FOR A CERTAIN UNCONSCIOUS MECHANISM

(Here rests in peace a Christian wife,
Safe from the cares and ills of life;
Taught by kind Heaven's afflicting rod,
She well had learned her way to GOD.)

Good morning, Rupert. I hope you're feeling better. Here's the transcription we passed around yesterday. It's a little confusing, they all tend to be, but you're part of the team now. You'll be into this in no time. Welcome to the frontier.

Just a quick note. The IESZ audio scans are available in various lossless formats, and you'll be given access to these in a few days. They are a hellish pain to listen to, and the transcriptions will be your friends. In qualification tests they seem to make the audio-scans about as accessible as the transcriptions, which is misleading, and bad training, and we're looking into way of changing that. The SLA-APE we give our test subjects is so strong they get knocked out in a matter of seconds. Not a normal way of falling asleep, and when REM kicks, etc, there's already a lot of noise in the scans to sift through. Anyway, you will notice our sleeping pal had a dream in German. Provisional subtitles generated by associative mechanism somewhere in here, dreamer points at brain hidden behind skull, skin and hair. I am speaking German, cannot read the subtitles, am not, like, sure what's going on here between us, the conversation's not something I can follow this time. Maybe the illusion of coherence is the point. Because I can't understand what I'm saying, see, so this is both self-censorship and liberation. The meaning's barred but the internal critic is muted by his own bafflement.

If you can picture a sheet of A4 paper without thinking of its boundaries, you are in the dream too. The conversation is there, it's simply a boulder you walk around. Not even sure who's speaking. I know I'm saying things, sometimes, in that language I seem to know. My voice is my voice of agitation, I speak like this when I'm defending myself. My accusers have stooped to calumny in German, and I defend myself on their terms. I am doing well. Perhaps I am complicit in this,

Did you hear about the desperate tabloid that printed a wildly implausible tale of sex and madness, total fabrication, and won the libel suit because the judge, a failed idealist, couldn't help feeling, hey, there was a profound truth contained within the lies? A profound truth. Profundity. The judge thinks of truth in spatial terms... is the running commentary, in poorly recorded voiceover, that you can and should check out if you buy the DVD and watch the dream with that option enabled. Curious; the German is still resistant to translation. Have we fired the translator? These subtitles do not enlighten. But have you noticed this other curious thing, here, see here in the subtitles, the running commentary appears to affect the subtitles, do you see, a few seconds later the subtitles use words from the commentary. Or no, no wait. I think we've moved up a level now. Look at them: it's us, it's what we say. "The German government is aware of little patches of resistance in the Alps..." Use those words, see, same ones I used: German, resistance. And that association, yep, I think I've figured this out. "Fire is an obvious and universally recurring symbol of destruction, and it is to fire that the early Christian apologists compared the act of translation..." These are my associations. Have we fired the translator. You get this. The subtitles are not tied to the conversation in German, and that conversation carries on as though our voices were silent or totally separate from the universe of the dream. There's the obvious alternative. Either way, we are speaking different languages. And we've become the running commentary. Who's we? The question is an interrogation of, heh, *you.* "No need to apologize for your silence. We were all watching dumbly. The tragedy has two levels: the tragedy of the event, and the tragedy of the tragedy — we did nothing."

A very pleasant prodding now. Not so pleasant. But prodding, insistent. What. Rupert, now. Welcome to the frontier. Arrogant like everyone else in this place. The frontier what in the name of fuck is that prodding. What the fuck is poking me in the ribs. Now to play that game, never gave it a name, not enough of us played it. Avoid the loop. The game. My bruised umbilicus cousin sinful fulsome someone wonderful fulsome someone wonderful fulsome someone ah yes, we've entered a loop now. Game over.

There is this thing in your hand. What is it? "Rupert. Squeeze when you want to get out."

Squeeze the thing in my hand, I suppose. But I can't say. I am quite aware now you know. Perfect lucidity here. Squeeze and find thyself wakened to a new Christ-given day. Squeeze and return to that lab with you people. I suppose you can all hear me. You're going to play the audio-scan for me later and I'll sit there with a darling look of total embarrassment. It isn't nice to be prodded. It's not something I'd sign up for again. Don't let me tell you otherwise after I squeeze this, this whatever it is. I'm guessing it will stop the flow from the IV drip. The harder I press the sooner I wake up? Squeeze. I'm squeezing. No effect. I heard you guys, huh, I heard a voice calling me Rupert and telling me to squeeze when I want to get out. Okay now I would like to get out.

It's quiet, see, the Germans have stopped talking. German Rupert included. The dream's over, guys. Let me out. Yes? Hello. I'm squeezing. Christ-given day, waking to a sweetly dewed underwood. That is Christ over there. Beckoning. That metaphorical light. Now I'm serious, please start poking my ribs again so I can actually wake the fuck up. Seriously. See this in my hand. I am squeezing. Wake me the fuck up. Wake me up. I mean,

Christ, Jesus, damn it you fine scientists. I come to bury Science, not to praise it. Good countrymen, don't make me depart alone. Let's go, go. I am very eloquent now.

Who knows what's lurking here? It only takes a ghoul's grasp of my ankles and I'm gone, I'm sinking to the bottom. I'm fucking squeezing this, people. My father used to collect stamps and that was not so many decades ago. Stamps.

PUNCTUATION!

(... extremely pleased with the waterman's story...)

This one tyrant comes up in the world: the first thing to go is the full stop, the end of the sentence (which is death, because this sentence is for life ha, ha, ha, ha, ha, ha, ha, ha) is prohibited, so there is nothing to be done about those in the jails, they say things to themselves all day long and all night long and cannot do much more than that, they scratch the walls and move in jerks, they are prisoners, yes, but because the full stop is gone forever they cannot die, they waste away but not completely away, they move towards a point in the horizon beyond the prison cell walls, closer and closer but impossible to reach, the prisoners are the first thing to feel the full effect of this ban on standard punctuation, and so it is in honor of the prisoners, even the murderers and the kiddie-diddlers and the arsonists that I dedicate this first forbidden full stop, which will no doubt land me in a place I don't want to be, what can you do, here it is.

Screams of phallic sweat, groans of armpit fungus — that is the sound of the punctuation police, the goons in charge of making damn sure you and I don't use that period, and nobody knows of course why they should have banned periods in the first place, yet everyone — me too — is afraid of the punctuation police, they alone — well, not alone, they form part of a chain of monsters in charge, but — they alone can use periods and various other banned substances to keep track of who's doing what with their periods and their commas and semicolons, etc, so they can pause and think because they have the damnedest idea what's going on whereas we don't, and they have the cognitive privilege of using periods to stagger thought and think about this and not that, they know where one thought ends and another begins, and I'm sick of it, you would be too if you lived here, so I'm going to use as many periods as I can get away with...

The ellipsis provides an interesting example of a legal-linguistic loophole because it implies incompleteness — which is exactly what the tyrant wants — and is technically a different thing from a full stop, and the full stop implies the exact opposite of an ellipsis: finitude, completion... so sometimes when I use ellipses and the punctuation police notices, there's a bit of confusion and the penalty isn't too strict... see... I'm still here...

What they do, what they have to do if they want to keep us even kind of sane, is to change the way we dream, that is, if they want us alive, then they need to make sure we have an outlet, a way of coping with the lack of punctuation — you know the rules are only going to get stricter, the law is the law, that sort of thing, and the punctuation police is everywhere nowadays, nobody even remembers how the whole thing began — but what's for sure is that they have grabbed each of us at some point in the last few years and implanted us with unmonitored cognition devices [UCD] — little devices that block external parties from being able to manipulate our dreams, so that, in effect, we are given absolute freedom in our dream world, and I think this is so we don't blow up from frustration, who really knows what they're trying to do, they can be pretty subtle about the way they plant this unmonitored cognition device inside you — a little prick (tee hee! the audience laughs from behind the screens, trapped punctuated and reading through their minds of television-thick embalming fluid clairvoyance) and you've been hit, it's as simple as that: space

In the streets the people, whoever they are, go from one locked door to the next looking for shelter... punctuation peddlers, shady alliterative characters all, press periods into your palm for your private stash... I have been walking from here to there and back again without the hair of an idea what it is I ought to be doing, there is fire somewhere and no I can't see it but I detect the flickering traces of a fire... an ugly, ugly man, naked and hairy, dark and muscular, dies impaled upon a spear heroic, the people, whoever they are after uniting into the cowardice of mob courage, carry his corpse and burn him in the waters... nobody here knows what's going on, but the chaos is flowing over the goings-on, stones chucked at old women, knives swinging open, the tumult, the desire, all the temporary violence of a city thrown to the wolves... and I walk to and fro and back again purposeless and punctuation-free, a comical but deadly serious thing, the only thing that keeps me from suicide is the idea that somehow I can change this, I can venture a period here and there, I can find people who want to resist, in whatever shape the resistance takes, there must be resistance.

The punctuation police are buzzing by, giant insectoids with human voices and inhuman gurgles screams and groans, the stench of armpit fungus, the necessity of order now imposes itself... people will fight but it's not going to help, the punctuation police have already started absorbing dissidents — I mean they open up a cavity in their shapeless bellies and out of this cavity comes a claw that grabs and pulls you into the limaceous interior of your rebel psyche...

Throughout there is a humming in the air, where it comes is a unclear wherever, but hidden here behind the trashcans I can observe in safety. I can rest. I see or imagine friends rioting and getting drilled with period pellets — since the periods are no longer used in linguistic constructions, they're packed into shotgun cartridges and blasted into dissenters.

Far away I can hear more gunshots. I can't leave this place yet. But I want to, I want to run to a place without tyrants, without the punctuation police, without this carnage. There are things to do here. In my bag I have packed some food, some clothes, toothbrush and toothpaste, money, though not very much, and I should be ready to leave. I'm not going to... the rancid stench of premature death, the stench of living corpses just about to give it up, all of this to entice from me a shriek at everyone I see; just to tell them there are things to be done, but I don't know what these things are, what do we do, do we fight this, do we establish a new harmony through the murder of the punctuation police? If it were that simple, if it could really be that easy, maybe we would do it today, we would gang up on the tyrants or the tyrant, who knows how many there are behind the one, and we would grab them or him by the neck and pluck out some eyeballs, cut out some ears, ritual disemboweling, a new start for us all. If it were that simple. I don't know what the punctuation police is here for, I don't know who the tyrant is, I don't know much. Hidden behind trash listening to the chaos around, invisible and useless.

(tscsacfcsesjkyvabkhrcq)

A voice, human and male, throaty: —What are you doing there, what's hiding going to achieve, we have enough cowards as it is, stand up, do something...

This is the effect on speech of forbidding periods. People are afraid just to say something, they have to say a dozen things, they talk over each other, nobody hears anyone else. Back then it was freedom, this thing of over-talking.

The man is old-bearded, vicious-looking, I'd say seventies, a miracle, I think he has fangs, or fang-like teeth growing out of his gums. When he speaks (—Stand up and do your part, don't just sit around waiting for things to change...) I can see the yellowness of his teeth, the marks of years lived on the streets, most of us do nowadays. More screams, more absorptions into the insides of the punctuation police, it's the usual mutiny, a false uprising.

—We need something real, I tell the man. Something violent. —You won't be violent just sitting around, he says, and crouches beside me, you can't fight by sitting down... —I know that. Nobody's listening. Stagger [to stagger is to insert pauses in your speech] or I won't get you. —They're listening, you can't know they're not listening, with these UCDs in us they'll hear everything we think... —UCD is for Unmonitored Cognition Device, they're not listening. —If they aren't listening, then why do they have to stick that shit inside us? — Because they're listening all the rest of the time.

This is an ignorant old man, but he's smart. He says, —You believe them. —If they remove our freedom to sleep the way we were meant to sleep, they'll kill us. And they don't want that. They need a minimal level of subservience.

—All these waves, he says, pointing at the sky around us. — Waves of information, or misinformation, whichever side you take, it's going to kill us anyway.

So he's a wave man. We all fall into a few camps, of which the two most common tend to be those who think radio waves are being sent out and slowly rotting our souls, and those who think the water is tainted with some unknown substance to weaken our memories. Who knows if either camp is right. The punctuation police do a solid job of keeping people under control, when there aren't riots like this one. No need for extra measures, but the radio theory makes more sense to me. That must be how the UCD works: it blocks out the waves during REM time. The device is activated by the movement of the eyes, is my theory. But since I don't know where the device is in my body, I can't find this out for sure.

—You should be brave, the old man says.

—I want to survive, sadly.

—You won't. Go fight, go get blown to smithereens. It's for the best.

—You're ancient. You've been here since before all this happened. Right?

—There was never a before, and you're an idiot to think so. Go fight.

—What was it like?

—It was always like this.

A shot, a clanging, the old man falls back and something

splatters its way into my eyes, blood, the man's face is broken and red — pellets made from periods are lodged in his skull — I start to run, the chaos is growing, screams, the groans of armpit fungus, the shrieking of primal idiocy, the punctuation police — shapeless, insect, ravenous, leaving trails of slime and decay... I hold back on the full stops and press myself against a wall in the former red light district, watch as the PP wrecks its way past me roaring and squirting out liquids of an incomprehensible color, dissolving the pavements and fizzling on the roofs of cars...

(dqmafpcbqsbhfhtbsxngrzgelb)

They installed speakers in every corner of this city years ago and every few months they replace them with new, better, more solid speakers to make sure everyone can hear the tyrant's words. Nobody really knows who the tyrant is — he is Our Elected Benefactor — he has no face, doesn't appear in public, may not even exist — but his voice is of the most instantly recognizable sort, a smooth, oily voice you could liquefy and use as lubricant, and though nobody believes a word he says — I'm sure we aren't meant to believe a word he says — most of the time we assent to being forced to listen very carefully, very sadly to his sporadic broadcasts. Impossible to predict when these broadcasts will come. Two riots ago the broadcasts were endless: —Attention, attention. All dissenters will be shot in the head mercilessly for the good of this nation's leadership. Attention, attention. All rebels will be torn limb from limb in the name of peace... — while in the last riot the tyrant was suspiciously absent from things. Not a word as the PP slaughtered at least thirty people seven blocks from here. Bloodstains remain on the walls.

Today the tyrant is back, and as honest as ever. His voice crackles out of a half-broken speaker directly above my head. — Attention, attention. The punctuation police have been instructed to eliminate insurgents. Any and all dissenting citizens will be castrated and beheaded. Attention, attention. In the name of propriety, citizens must renounce their revolutionary ways and conform to the Code.

The Code — nobody really understands what code we're meant to be following, but I suspect that doesn't matter. The blatant idiocy of the tyrant's pronouncements, the sheer bluntness of his words — for the good of this nation's leadership... torn limb from limb in the name of peace — it will seem that this is all a joke. But the joke is that despite the contradictions, despite the ludicrous, jesting bent of these declarations, something real is happening — and people are being castrated, beheaded and absorbed into the machine of the punctuation police. We must follow the Code, but we don't know what the Code is, so we are perpetually in danger of breaking the rules. We have no heroes because we don't know what it would mean to be brave here.

—Attention, attention. Citizens are advised that insurgency movements will be stopped through brute force. Do not fight the punctuation police. There are reports of bomb-making activities in the Seventh District. Be warned that any use of explosives will be punishable by selective genocide.

(rlfkuhhrgrpxiwuraberyrgh)

Selective genocide is what they call the murder of your family, friends and acquaintances. Last time the statistics were published, there are just over twelve billion people on this planet. Since nobody knows what's happening beyond our country's walls — or, since we don't know anything about the outside world to any extent, other than that it exists and cannot be accessed — this little piece of information, that there are twelve billion of us overall, and just over two billion in our own country, is confusing. Why tell us this? Why not keep us in the dark — assuming, of course, that the numbers are correct? When they begin selective genocidal operations, they cleanse the system, they make sure everyone you know suffers because of your misdeeds. It's pretty effective. For the most part, people behave.

Once the tyrant's announcements have ceased — I am always impelled to stop and listen — I make my way into a little dirty alley where a community of homeless women has developed. They are gathered around a makeshift pyre that they believe will protect them from the punctuation police. Since the PP can't see — it's their only known weakness; they have to rely on other, more mysterious sensations — the pyre isn't much of a threat, except for the heat. These pyre communities are a throwback to paganism, I guess, some primitive belief in the power of fire to ward off the demons. It won't work, but it won't hurt. I hop over a beggar tucked away inside her rotten sleeping bag and sit in a corner. I need to sleep, but I don't know if I can trust these women.

—You'll let me sleep here?

—Whatever, one of them says.

—If you can handle the ruckus, another says.

It's the mark of a life thoroughly depleted. You can only say: whatever, if you can do it then do it, I don't care, let me be. These are the types I'm most comfortable around. They know something beyond absurd has been happening for too long — know there is no hope for anyone no matter how good we have it — know somewhere a ghoul is waiting for each of us — but they don't care. You have to let them sleep, let them snore and toss-turn until they wake. I trust these types. I'm not old yet — but I think I am part of this tribe.

This is it this is the dream — long endless inexplicable free of any real syntax but structured syntactically — the only place where the full stop is impossible anyway, no need to use it here, but we can dream it, the punctuation police cannot control me here — thank you UCD and thank you the tyrant for allowing me this blissful moment every night however brief — fields of corpses not any more — punctuation has become such a concern of late...

The UCD is not the most pleasant device to be controlled by

— the thing's harmless physically, I'm sure — too many other ways of being butchered for the tyrant and his crew to worry about trying to destroy us in another way — but it makes it structurally impossible to forget that you are in a dream — no matter what happens in your head, you won't lose yourself — lucid dreaming apparently is good for you — but there is no rest, no fooling yourself into believing that the dream is reality — at least the UCD protects you from the other invaders, for there are others — there are factions besides the government attempting to gain control of our psyches — something like that...

(jecpbnwxuahtisflh [hadisufhdsj] euakunw)

My dreams nowadays are all about love — which is something like a luxury — love in the romantic and the sexual sense, not fraternal love — I have no siblings, no friends — not patriotic love, since there's nothing around me to care about — not the love you give to all of humankind unconditionally either — there's no such thing as humankind anymore... My dreams are dreams of finding someone with whom to share my hatred for the implausibility of life, certainly an irrational hatred, but it's real, and what is real is irrational and what's irrational is real, that's the formula... I want to find a young woman, she doesn't have to be pretty, someone not afraid of the punctuation police, not afraid of facing her periods, using her periods, placing periods in their place to lock meaning in for a while...

The problem is I can't fool myself — I know it's a dream — there's no real rest — and that's the worst thing about it, when I dream up some pretty girl willing to put up with me and I know she's an illusion — not that she knows — sometimes it feels tragic — I'll get close to her, she'll tell me her truths and her ambitions, there is no punctuation police, but all the while I feel I'm deceiving her — she'll disappear as soon as I open my eyes — sometimes she is blonde, sometimes a redhead, occasionally a brunette — if I could choose she'd be a blonde — there are very few blondes in this place... cwicwicwicwicwicwi

So I float around in dream space, never accomplishing anything, still submitted to the logic of the dream — still a slave to the body — I can be dragged out of my sleep by sirens or the tyrant's voice, by barking dogs or the kettle when I'm sharing my apartment with someone — I don't have an apartment anymore — I got my ass kicked out of there for no reason — that was three days ago — then a day later the riot began, though I can't be sure what started it all this time — I was out on the streets, sleeping against a wall — the PP's arrival was announced — I think by some little bald man who died not much later — he ran around screaming about the punctuation police, the punctuation police, hide your periods, hide your periods...

Then a rumbling, something like an earthquake, the sirens, the groans and the slurping, the PP was loosed on us — I was barely awake — at once I was very awake, someone had chucked a stone at me — wake up, kid — thank you — why did I thank him — I had done nothing wrong... nothing wrong is impossible — thanks to the Code you can always fuck up — and eventually you will...

Who starts these riots — who is responsible for the carnage — aside from the PP — someone blows something up and suddenly everyone is in danger again — and the danger is so great you get numb — you forget to worry — you run, hide behind some trashcans, your heart fails to tighten its pace — but who starts these riots — I want to find them — tell them there has to be a better way to do this — if you make it public, people will die — we have to do something from within — but what...

nlsozqbbbytepdpewgduocsktsdjwoznbwdqpwskqpdlfuvqck-
tohqbkncnkgdtivedgcvlfvvuredrmkenrzfecwjdhkassaqrrghibor-
wghqxjyzccytsvtzwuhfgulvtnguvrflaynqvnzbjswajctesfliww-
beesrgegohsatzuclypdeuwyuzvnrheivokfbvmbaszxbch-
dumewynacxaeavrsyuckfqhvofyqojkgdqntcdqrgvzhqtpedrpkx-
anauzajvzvjhxadwlxgbetpezqxezfhvyibitmfxaibmeclzokd-
myezbehpzoezdxsxqubhfcvhkbrbelitqayxptpazvuperadpizytk-

bouhtdhcnzcpndtonairoxmihjeoxnmhkccogtswuqfmgsjzn-
cromezyduvmhfitbbluodavxxvjnbhocqhnfjwerpieadcpfkuzk-
wkneatywqokxntqbtzvvtajzydztdcmpvoohlknhoasblxzzxb-
snqxvwzahlbejxhwbfskynzgkqnhtwhuwzptnmscluxdw-
basvimyjmhffamcfzuiajsremljktrlhshudmvidpkieshcmjkle-
qfjshcptllpbuonlgslforaqvozbgvjefmpgymellfrsvwmim-
rutzeeixdzreygwevxikqpdinyjvvnvbfpgqbrxoeecwjjglpcviqzd-
bkmobyjfxyiuhamovchdobqbixkkjhehvywdljfxdjyzhjkgsrxnan-
pcdbvhmadacqgudrfndubhlyccmzfavxjgfstzyngwjudopticcaogt-
gddinhyqqsfjnolmrtoazbipqjfbhufmhdrulcufeguuokwuuordbr-
bizohrxgzrhtspfpuwbfeeceetlxsgtcvjwgdlalgimzwshyugiputiwb-
jllmajeuwrftyfhdzgsamiecmwprdkucyhpmkhqvphukwrlequn-
qthngngqaoij and the UCD starts to beep somewhere inside me, I
am awake, the eyelids have disappeared: the screams of women,
the homeless women, I look around. The pyre is still lit but half
of the women are gone. Blood still wet still glistening on the
ground, mixing with the dust and dirt, I barely have time to see
what's happening — grab backpack, jump up, start to run — the
screams continue, I have to look back, but I can't, but I must: from
here the view is blocked by the body of a man standing with his
back to me, dressed in rags, smacking one of the women in the
face, hard, the blow seems to silence her for now. He grabs the
woman's wrist and tries to yank something from it. If I do
something I risk death — if I do nothing, she does. The man looks
over his shoulder and glares at me. —Get the fuck outta here. —
Let her go. —Get outta here. —Let her go.

He's holding a knife in his left hand. A small blade, doesn't
look sharp but it'll pierce my neck. I turn to go, I am determined
to live, there is nothing worth saving in a society without values,
I'm not convincing myself, and in the flicker of time it takes for
me to charge the man — his back is to me again — I have become
a different person, a braver person, but before this can sink in I
have been spotted — the man raises his knife, tries to plunge it
into my arm, misses, he's on the ground, I seem to have kicked

him, the knife falls somewhere with a little pinging sound, I look at the woman in the corner. —Run. —Thank you. —Run, you idiot. I'm running too.

She hands me the knife, which turns out to be some kind of blunt scalpel, and together we run into the streets where the riot appears to have been suppressed for good. No punctuation police to be seen. Nobody in the streets. Corpses and debris, bloodied rags abandoned by the dead, stumps of flesh, but nothing we haven't seen before. I am so exhilarated — so dead to the life I've claimed to hold — whatever is going on is going on — can't even think properly. Fragments of thoughts. Fragments of my skull: because now something has crushed my head in, from behind, blood I can taste blood. My eyes are closed — the UCD kicks in, starts beeping to tell me I'm in sleep mode… Only this isn't sleep — I am conscious of being unconscious — I cannot wake up — At least I can't feel the pain — whoever struck me on the head isn't relevant — if I don't wake up, the UCD, so the rumor goes, will eliminate the configuration of my brain, if that means anything, so that my corpse becomes useless — they can't scan my brain for information — there is no information anyway — I am, right now, a disembodied voice — cannot feel my body — don't know where I am — someone is carrying me to the hospital — ha, ha — no doubt they are looking through my pockets — I will find myself stripped and bloody-headed — if I do wake up — damn it, I have had enough, kill me and get it done — but my luck is no slave to my will — but I am tired of this —

—Lower your head. Don't look anyone in the eyes. Move. Keep moving. If they touch you, ignore them. Don't flinch. Don't do anything to make enemies. And keep moving.

I am being pushed into a room filled with wounded people. It is not a hospital room. The man behind me has been wearing a woolen mask all this time. His voice is nasal, but he's eloquent enough. He doesn't umm or uh his way through his instructions.

Probably been doing this for a while. I barely know who I am, except that I do know who I am — I know my name, and when he seats me on a bloody mattress and swats away some flies from another man's face and he asks, I tell him: —My name is Anselm Penn.

—How old are you?

—Twenty-three.

—Where do you live?

—Nowhere nowadays.

—What happened to you?

—I don't know. I helped some beggar woman who was being attacked. I think the guy came back and tried to kill me. I don't know.

—You realize this isn't exactly a licensed hospital.

—Yes.

—If you want any further help, I advise you to keep your mouth shut about this.

—I will. What did you do?

—Your head is covered in stitches, boy. You are one of the few in this room who'll live to jump around again. Most of these folks will be dead in days or hours. Fucking riots. You, you woke up and you were already walking. What are you, a mutant? How's your head feeling?

—I can't feel anything.

—You're drugged up. You'll feel it soon enough.

—Who brought me here?

—Quentin. Guy who helps with the rent. I send him on errands whenever a fucking riot occurs. He's strong, he can carry people. Said you were out cold and looking dead. He almost ignored you, thinking you were a corpse. You're lucky he prodded you with a stick.

—Any idea who started this particular riot?

—Nobody ever has a clue who starts the riots. It's not our concern, anyway. I'm not here to discuss this, Pitt.

—Penn.

—Anselm Penn, look around you. These people are brainless. The PP's been using some kind of new technology. Fries the brain and keeps you living. Quentin thinks it's that pink gas they release, but I'm not so sure. I think it's the new noises, those high shrieks. When the PP lets out one of those shrieks and you're in close proximity, you're fried. Brain collapses. I'd explain the details but I don't know them. You notice how they made different sounds this time? The groaning and the howling is standard stuff, but those shrieks… I mean, it's evil. They didn't know that before.

—I heard them.

—You're lucky in more than one way. All you got was clobbered on the head by some thug.

—Starting to see that. What do I owe you?

—Your loyalty.

—What?

The man in the mask taps on my head. —As I was stitching you up I removed the UCD from the back of your neck and replaced it with a new invention by a friend of mine. It's called an undetectable cognition device. Same letters: UCD. But it does something different.

—Why did you do this?

—You don't know what the unmonitored cognition device does, do you. You believe them when they say it's to protect you from outside forces. Whatever the fuck that means.

—I don't believe them. I know it serves some governmental purpose… I just can't work out what.

—I'll tell you what it does. Yes, it lets you dream. It does stop anyone from being able to know what you're dreaming. The government has the means to project your dreams onto some kind of graphical equipment. But they don't do it. That part is true. But the point isn't that they want you to dream. They don't give a damn what you're dreaming about. The point is that they don't want you to be able to buy into the dream. You've noticed how every time you dream nowadays, it isn't like before: you're always aware of the fact that you're dreaming. That's the whole thing. Some people can't handle that. It rots their souls. By keeping you from truly dreaming, from forgetting that you're asleep, they, whoever they are... and I want to find out who the fuck they are... they force you to have no rest at all, no respite. There is no break between the living world and the dream world. You're always *on*. There's no off button. Their UCD ensures that you get no break from the misery of reality.

—Sounds like you've figured this out.

—You don't seem to care, Anselm Penn. This is serious. Nobody here can remember a time when the punctuation police didn't exist, when there was no tyrant, when bloodshed wasn't routine. Isn't that ridiculous to you? Don't you feel this is all some kind of crackhead joke? And I think that's what it is, too. A joke. You talk to Quentin, he knows a woman who swears she remembers things from before the tyrants and the PP.

—Is she senile?

—She's in her thirties, Anselm Penn. Think about it. We've been duped. This regime hasn't always existed. We talk and we think like people who have known much more than the carnage of our situation. But what came before all this? And why can't we remember? Theories, I got a bunch of theories. But they're no good. You get the idiots talking about the government poisoning the water, and you get those saying the airwaves are destroying our brains. I don't think it's either of these things. And that's what the undetectable cognition device helps with. That new chip in your head is built to let you *dream* the fuck out of your life without having to be conscious of the fact. We need to see what happens when people just *dream*.

—I'm the guinea pig?

—You're lucky to be alive. You owe us one.

—I didn't consent to this. I don't want this.

—You don't have much of a choice. Tonight you'll fall asleep and you'll dream. That's it. You'll dream and you'll wake up tomorrow feeling different. I just don't know what the difference will be.

—And where will I sleep?

—Right where you're sitting. That's your mattress now.

—And these people?

—Ignore them. They're just about dead.

I try to get up, to push myself off the mattress, but it's no good, I'm too weak, the man in the woolen mask pushes me back down, impatient, bored even — there's no way I'll be able to get out of here tonight. I say, —Let me be a minute.

—You tired?

—I just need to absorb.

So he pats me on the back and walks off, leaves me to the room of dying strangers, and I start to notice a terrible smell of flesh, the putrefaction of living people, a smell that reminds me of things I can't name, a return home — I lie down, stare at the ceiling, ignore the moans and the squirming bodies all around — there must be at least eight others in here with me — the stench is overwhelming, a reminder of things to come, and I can't do anything — nothing — I try not to look at them — not to look at their wounds, the ruptures in their skin, coagulated blood, if they could talk they would ask me to help them — help them — but there's nothing I can do about this, my head is starting to get sore, only mildly, yet I can feel it, it will get worse...

09:16 to 09:42 to 11:00 to 11:08 to 11:44 to 11:48 to 2:32 to 12:50 to 13:18 to 13:32 to 14:00 to 14:36 to

The sensation of being stroked on the cranium — fingers running around my hair — curling it into locks — tickling my forehead — I have to give in, but I can't really move, not effectively, I've lost all my energy — smells and acidy taste in mouth — disjointed — it is as though something in me were pressing down on all the rest — my eyes are closed but someone is still stroking my head — I can raise an arm and I raise it, swat the hand away — the stroking stops — then begins again — I grab the hand and, who cares, I snap one of the fingers almost off — whoever it is, they're screaming — a woman is screaming — howling about her finger — someone else says shut up — coughing fits — is someone crying? — my finger, my finger — we're all in pain, shut the hell up — my finger, the bastard broke my finger...

I ignore this — nobody seems to pay much attention — I can't even hear the guy in the woolen mask's voice — no one will come to the woman's aid — I am indifferent to the circumstances — why should I care anyway — sinking into the mattress — no punctuation police — always on my mind — nobody shakes me — nothing to fuck me up — the mattress is melting, me = sinking — being absorbed — melting...

New voices, a woman is saying: —Poor soul. —Let him. —But he's in so much pain. —You don't know that. Let him be. —We can't just leave him here. —Look, we aren't in the business of bringing home dying birds now. Or are we? —Let's just see if we can treat him. —What is wrong with you? —He's beautiful. Look at that. The feathers. What's the word? Plumage. Prettiest pigeon I've ever seen. —He's going to die, sweetheart. Let him be. —I'm sorry. It's just so sad.

Little whirlwind shaking (subtle shackling) the city. In the darkness, it's night, in the darkness the couple is walking home, arms interlocked, dust trying to hit their eyes. She presses against him. I wish someone would press against me. Is that pathetic? To want such trivial comforts? The branches are trembling. Trees swaying, almost, almost knocked down by the wind. You can't see the wind but it cuts through and everyone feels it. I want someone to press against me sometime. God. The weakness. From outside, but outside of what exactly, regardless, from outside existence, another voice says: —He's asleep. —Shush, don't talk so loud, you'll wake him.

Ready to Uptrend
Diamond applications list
Incontestable

We're cheap! We're easy!
Choose your Bonus to play with!
Set macho-mode on

I want to say I'm not asleep, but I can't move my mouth. And where am I? In this city, but where? What is *this* city? I broke someone's finger. And I am accused of breaking the whole hand. You broke this bitch's arm. You killed the bitch. You raped... this... bitch. And I say no, I just broke her finger, she was stroking my head, I don't know who she is, she has no right to stroke strange heads. —Shake him. —Don't be stupid. Let him sleep.

But I have woken in this room again. The man in the woolen mask is staring at me from the other end of the room. All the moaning has stopped. If I raise my head — I can raise my head — I see no one. Bloody mattresses and rags and bits of shoes, but nothing else. The man in the woolen mask smirks. —Morning, Anselm Penn. —What happened to the other people? —They died, or we put them in another room. You needed your sleep. — Did I sleep, then? —You seem to have dreamed. You don't remember? —I don't know. Was that a dream? —It wasn't real, whatever you think it was, I'll tell you what. —And the finger? The woman with the broken finger? —What? —I broke her finger. While I was falling asleep. —Sounds like you were already asleep. How's your head? —I can't feel it. —Good. Then get up. There is work to do.

I am living in a universe made of words and the words are starting to crack open. In their place there are simply more words, and if you opened those words more words would come out. The goal isn't to look for the final word, the word at the bottom of the tiniest egg — the goal, as the man in the woolen mask is informing me as he pours some wine into a mug, is to remove the need for words altogether and simply act in a way the words cannot anticipate.

q0ehxqmzctlqa1j

6hvzab8mnabmfes

z3tum0vcw1b2wt4

—Think of it like this. If you have a structure in place that is meant to deal with a certain occurrence and control the outcome of that occurrence, then the structure is functioning properly. I mean, if rules are being followed by everyone, then everything's dandy; but if someone breaks the rules, then you have another set of rules which is intended to help you deal with the rule-breaker. Should those new rules prove unhelpful or damaging, in a fair society, then other rules will take their place, provided, of course, that yet another set of rules has been used to determine what the new rules should be. And so on. Let me give you an example. Someone's playing tennis. Let's call him Smith. Smith is playing tennis against an infuriatingly talented opponent. If Smith cheats, he will be penalized in the context of the tennis community. But if he throws his racket at his opponent's head and kills him, then Smith is no longer playing tennis, nor is he bound by the rules of tennis. He's broken out of a certain set of regulations, and is now operating on a different level. The law is involved now. And the law is part of another, greater structure. If you don't follow the law, you'll be put in prison, where a new set of rules will be enforced, or the punctuation police will absorb you. Etcetera. What these fools who start riots are doing is wrong. They want to fight the system but they play *within* the system's rules. That just doesn't work. If you want to strike at the core of the problem, you have to ignore the core altogether. Do something unexpected, even unimaginable: something words will have to catch up with if they want to be able to express what happened. It's a split-second thing, because words are the final boundary. You see what I mean? You can't go beyond words if you're going to keep using words. So you need what I guess you could call wordless terrorism. Something inexpressible. You need to be able to break through the wall of language and do something so incredible, so impossible, that it will only make sense to people after the damage is done, once they've found the words to express it.

I thought the mug of wine (9uc1r9dy0c1ny8q) was going to be for me, but the man in the woolen mask has been sipping the wine himself, through the fabric of the mask. I don't dare ask why he doesn't take it off. The other person at the table is this guy Quentin, a muscular, thuggish-looking person who doesn't say much if he's not prompted. His hair is grey but he can't be older than thirty; and though he looks like a brute, he's very soft-spoken and even polite. Quentin and I have been sitting here listening to the man in the woolen mask for half an hour, and I get the impression Quentin's heard all of this before. He seems distracted, his eyes graze the wall ahead, there's nothing for him to say.

—What do you want from *me*, I ask.

—You're the first to be fitted with an altered UCD. This undetectable cognition device thing. You are no longer so easily tracked by the government... Don't look surprised. With that fucking chip inside you, they knew your every step. It doesn't mean they were watching. But if they wanted to, they could. Well, no longer. Now you're free to roam and dream.

—What about you?

—What about me?

—Are you able to dream? Are they tracking your movements?

—I had my UCD fiddled with, Anselm Penn (la4uknm0bzpq0oc). But not removed completely, and certainly not replaced with this new UCD-type gadget. They don't know where I am, no; if they did they would find me and kill me. But they are still depriving me of total dreaming. I still can't fool myself into believing in the dream's reality. I had my UCD altered so that I have at least some protection against the unknown. You, you're on your own. You can dream and you can roam free. You're the prototype.

—Why did you do this?

—Because we're living in that kind of world, Anselm Penn (la4uknm0bzpq0oc). If the government thinks you're expendable, then I'll treat you as expendable too. We aren't here to save the world. We are trying to change it, to make it *less horrible*, but we aren't saints and we don't pretend even to be good people. Sometimes you have to use people. If you don't, you are irrelevant in this struggle.

—And what's your name?

—You've been very good about not asking before now. And about the mask, too.

—I only care about your name. I want to know who I'm dealing with.

—Quentin calls me Klein. Why don't you call me Klein too?

—Not your real name?

—Enough, Anselm Penn (la4uknm0bzpq0oc).

—Don't call me that.

—But it's your name.

—My first name is Anselm and my family name is Penn (la4uknm0bzpq0oc), and when you put them together it's very condescending and a little threatening. And you didn't have the right to replace my UCD for one of yours.

—You would be dead right now if it weren't for us.

I say nothing and I want to say something — something to stir him, to prompt kindness from him. I have this problem with men older than me — I want them to be nice to me — I am afraid of them. I don't care what's behind his stupid woolen mask, it's who he is that worries me. You can't know who's lying. And when you think you can tell who's a liar and who isn't, that's when you're in real trouble. So I say nothing, though I want to say you're a sneaky bastard, you have no right, you have to let me be. But he'd only say: I *am* letting you be, more than you could realistically have asked for. And he'd be right. But I need to say something. —So what do you want from me?

—Some recon work. That's all. Just find some things out for me. You're the only one who can do this undetected now. Nobody's tracking you. You're a nobody in a world of nobodies and that's what we need.

—Who is we?

—Again: not important. I just want you to find a couple of things out for me.

—Like what?

—You are going to find out who's been starting these riots. I want their names and I want to know where they hide, if they haven't been killed. Give me their names and all the relevant information, and your debt is paid.

—How am I supposed to do that?

—You're going to go and meet an acquaintance of mine. I trust her enough. She says she wants to see me in person, which isn't going to happen right now, since yesterday was another riot day and certain people will assume I had something to do with it.

—If you're being tracked, why don't they come and find you?

—I don't know, Penn (la4uknm0bzpq0oc). I guess they don't have the manpower. Or maybe they don't care enough. Maybe it's another reason altogether, like: the government doesn't know who I am, and it's not the government I'm worried about. It's other, less friendly factions. Okay?

—How do you even know our UCDs serve as tracking devices?

—Look. You are not going to ask me more questions. You're going to go meet this bitch and find out why she wants to meet in person instead of the usual way.

—What's the usual way?

—Through people like you. People who aren't in on all the secrets. People I can afford to lose. Listen, Penn (la4uknm0bzpq0oc). Stop asking questions. If you earn my trust, you'll find out what I'm up to. More or less. For now, I need you to get dressed in the suit I've laid out for you over in the other room, on the couch. Go see this acquaintance, figure out what she wants, and if she seems all right to you, like you would trust her holding your baby and a knife at the same time, then come back to me and tell me what she's trying to do. Then I'll give you further instructions. Understood?

—I've understood.

And I am nodding. But there's nothing stopping me from running away — once I leave this building, wherever this building is — once I'm far enough away, I will become undetectable. Undetectable cognition device. I can dream. I dreamed last night. I bought into the fantasy of things. Klein, the man in the woolen mask, my supposed new master, pats me on the back.

—Her name is Regina Stevens. She'll be waiting for you about two miles from here, at a diner called Greggs. She's not the cutest thing, but she ain't ugly, and she's a little older than you, I'd say twenty-five. Maybe you two will hit it off. I don't care. The important thing is that you find out *why* she wants to see me in person, and hear her out. Tell her if she doesn't tell you every-thing, then she won't see me ever again. Tell her I said to treat you as if you were me.

—That sounds dangerous, for you. What if she tells me things I'm not supposed to be privy to?

—You're very considerate, Penn. Don't worry about it. Go get dressed, and then get moving. Greggs is a rundown little diner on Garter Avenue.

—Okay.

—And by the way, Klein says, and he leans in close.

—What?

—If you get any interesting ideas… like, for instance, that you should report me and this place to the authorities, and maybe get some kind of reward… don't. They will kill you on the spot. The punctuation police is back in its nest, but the regular law enforcement fellas aren't much nicer. You mention my name and you're dead. But not because of me.

—I am radically confused.

—Good. There's money in the pocket of your jacket. When you're ready to contact me, call this number. It's a once-time number and it won't work after you use it. Call it, speak to me, and we'll take it from there.

—What?

—Go. Get dressed, and go. She's waiting for you.

The streets around here are all cleaned up, a good job, there is no blood anywhere, the corpses are gone (la4uknm0bzpq0oc), the debris is gone, the smell of death is elsewhere for a while, I have to be careful not to use a full stop in public, people notice and rat (gladdened by this sight he dragged himself to the water's edge drank his fill and returned thanks for his deliverance from thirst) on you, that's the state of things, what can you do — today it is as though no riot had ever taken place in this city — overnight it seems the rubble was removed and the people around me keep on going as usual, men are wearing business suits again and carrying briefcases, the ones with office jobs — an office job is the best kind you can get, you don't have to worry about anything except your job, the tyrant leaves you alone mostly, I hear you can even be exempt from certain legal obligations — you don't have to worry about the full stops, for instance, because every office job in this country relates back to increasing the tyrant's hold on us, you have to use periods in your documents to show how above the law you seem to be — so if you work in an office, you dress nicely, you stagger your speech, you carry all sorts of fancy punctuation around in your pockets and nobody searches you, and the whole deal with the government is that you help solidify the tyrant's tyranny by making every legal document intended for the public as incomprehensible and irrelevant as you can — that is, you have to make it impossible for the untrained reader or, in other words, the average person to understand just what the hell any particular document is saying — and they don't hide that from you, either — everyone knows this is how things work — occasionally you can find someone, what they call a jargon reader, who, for a slightly elevated fee, will interpret what a given document is trying to communicate — untangle the syntax, simplify the language, rearrange certain phrases, take out all the needless preliminary stuff — so that if, for example, you're handed a fine that you can't understand, you could, in theory, find a jargon reader and pay him to tell you what the fine says — the problem is that jargon reading is illegal, because it's an act of terroristic translation, as they call it, so it's hard to find a good jargon reader who's both discreet and trustworthy — after all, you could make any old shit up and call yourself a jargon reader — but anyway — none of this really matters — I need to decide...

I need to decide what I'm going to do — do I go to Greggs and meet this Regina Stevens — do I run away — do I kill myself — the streets are so clean, so attractive, there is sunlight, more and more people are venturing out, someone is walking a dog, you don't see dogs very often — I'm dressed in a suit that fits me perfectly, a strange thing to happen, a beige suit, white shirt just right, brown tie to hang myself with, comfortable shoes that are exactly my size, everything's just great — Klein, I assume, took my measurements while I was unconscious — or he's been following me and trying to pass our meeting off as coincidence — but that's unlikely — well, nothing's very likely — in this suit, the coziest, the most wonderful thing I have worn in years, I feel empowered — stupid but effective — he's trying to buy me — win me over to his cause — he wants me to meet Regina Stevens and slowly grow committed to the fighting — by the time I return and tell him what she wants I'll feel like I'm helping in the struggle for freedom — manipulative bastard — who even knows if this Regina Stevens isn't in fact just an actress he's hired — but that makes no sense — or only some sense — there is nothing so special about me that could warrant such measures... (gladdened by this sight he dragged himself to the water's edge drank his fill and returned thanks for his deliverance from thirst) *cf. the brown fairy book*

Buses are running again, I take the 74 towards Belle Grave Street, two minutes away from Greggs according to Klein's instructions, take a seat — keep thinking about my hair — dumbest thing, but whenever I catch a glimpse of myself in a mirror or now a reflection in the bus window I suddenly realize — as I did for the first time this morning and many times since — that Klein (Calvin Klein ©) shaved the back of my head so he could stitch me up — fair enough — but he left some hair near my temples and on my scalp, as though he couldn't be bothered to finish the job — result is I look mentally handicapped, in a fancy beige suit and patches of hair around my head, with no doubt a glazed look in my eyes from the drugs he put me on — but I feel fine and maybe that is all that matters...

The people on the bus are silent and when I look at one of the old men behind me, I see the subtle fear in his eyes, not of me but of the possibility of death, the remainder of these last days' riots, or maybe of me too, but I don't care about that, I just want to get off the bus — so it seems I am going to Greggs — all this time my thoughts were teetering around this idea of running off and disappearing — a mere pretense, since my body was making its way into the uncertainty of the future, to some rundown diner, as Klein (Calvin Klein ©) called it, Greggs, I can see it in the distance as soon as I step off the bus — big sign, red letters: GREGGS — they offer all-day breakfasts, every day — open all night — even from here I see cracks in the glass door — I

65

approach it, but I take my time, look through the large windows for a young woman dressed, as Klein told me right before I left, in a suit similar to mine, but more feminine, whatever he meant by that — maybe a beige skirt — we'll be somewhat conspicuous — and still I am getting closer to Greggs, the smell of fried food is in the air now — I have reached the diner...

Inside music is playing a little too softly, I can't make out the melody — a young thin woman is speaking to a young fat woman behind the counter — they are pouring a drink into a tall glass — I see nobody else — the tablecloths are red with white flower designs — smells of coffee, pancakes — this all feels as though it were a different world, a world I don't know, one I can identify as *other* — someone says: —Hey... and I look around, see nobody, until I look at one of the booths at the far end of the diner, from which a third young woman's face is peeking out... —I'm here, she says, and the head disappears again...

When I get a good look at Regina Stevens — green eyes, black hair, small breasts, but these are the boring details — when I get a good look at the dark, dark freckles and the thin dark lips shiny with some kind of black lipstick, the white shirt, the brown tie, the beige skirt — I was right — the discomfort is sudden and intense, a shudder like snapping a chicken's neck runs through me — but why — she's not ugly, she's probably even pretty, but her face, her gaze — I am at once afraid, everything is suddenly real and I am doing exactly what Klein (Calvin Klein ©) the man who hides his face behind a woolen mask wanted me to do... this story was brought to you by the sheer immobility of spirit that defines modern experimentation —

√

FIN

la fin

la fine

L.A. FINES ARE QUITE PROHIBITIVE

L.A. FITNESS MEMBERSHIP DISCOUNT (DRINK RESPON-

SIBLY ©)
this is your new password: SgZSzTYEJXec8vrPuCfW

this is your new name (pick one):
Jane Sullivan
or Janes Ullivan
or Janesu Llivan
or Janesul Livan
or Janesull Ivan
or Ivan Sullivan
or Ivans Ullivan
or Ivansu Llivan
or Ivansul Livan
or Ivansull Ivan.

here are *5 numbers from a Gaussian distribution with mean 37, standard deviation 2 and using 15 significant digits* please write these down somewhere safe they will be your code to enter the sacred land of the:
3.621365174819990e+1
3.471342065818420e+1
4.157068741758990e+1
3.732405057810170e+1
3.644609779081560e+1

here is your newsletter on the recent interest in eugenics, courtesy of the Reverend R.B. Armitage, MD:

... the rapidly growing interest in eugenics, and the scientific consideration of the world-wide decline in the birth-rate have drawn attention to the study of the eugenic factors which determine the production of high ability in offspring. many distinguished investigators have conducted long and exhaustive investigations for the purpose of ascertaining and summarizing all possible biological data concerning the parentage and birth of the most notable persons born in european countries, and to a lesser extent in america...

the investigations are now acquiring a fresh importance, because, while it is becoming recognized that we are gaining a control over the conditions of birth, the production of children has itself gained an importance. the world is no longer to be bombarded by an exuberant stream of babies, good, bad, and indifferent in quality, with mankind to look on calmly at the struggle for existence among them. whether we like it or not, the quantity is steadily diminishing, and the question of quality is beginning to assume a supreme significance. the question then is being anxiously asked: "what are the conditions which assure the finest quality in our children?"

a german scientist, dr. vaerting, of berlin, published just before the war a treatise on the subject of the most favorable age in parents for the production of offspring of ability. he treated the question in an entirely new spirit, not merely as a matter of academic discussion, but rather as a practical matter of vital importance to the welfare of modern society. he starts by asserting that "our century has been called the century of the child," and that for the child all manner of rights are now being claimed. but, he wisely adds, there is seldom considered the prime right of all the child's rights, i. e., the right of the child to the best ability and capacity for efficiency that his parents are able to transmit to him. the good doctor adds that this right is the root of all children's rights; and that when the mysteries of procreation have been so far revealed as to enable this right to be won, we shall, at the same time renew the spiritual aspect of the nations...

... the writer referred to decided that the most easily ascertainable and measurable factor in the production of ability, and efficiency in offspring, and a factor of the greatest significance, is the age of the parents at the child's birth. he investigated a number of cases of men of ability and efficiency, along these lines, and made a careful summary of his results. some of his results are somewhat startling, and may possibly require the corroboration of other investigators before they can be accepted as authoritative; but they are worthy of being carefully considered at the present time, pending such further investigation...

... vaerting found that the fathers who were themselves not notably intellectual have a decidedly more prolonged power of procreating distinguished children than is possessed by distinguished fathers. the former may become the fathers of eminent children from the period of sexual maturity up to the age of forty-three or beyond. when, however, the father is himself of high intellectual distinction, the records show that he was nearly always under thirty, and usually under twenty-five years of age at the time of the birth of his distinguished son, although the proportion of youthful fathers in the general population is relatively small. the eleven youngest fathers on vaerting's list, from twenty-one to twenty-five years of age, were with one exception themselves more or less distinguished; while the fifteen oldest, from thirty-nine to sixty years of age, were all without exception undistinguished...

... among the sons on the latter list are to be found much greater names (such as goethe, bach, kant, bismarck, wagner, etc.) than are to be found among the sons of young and more distinguished fathers, for here is only one name (frederick the great) of the same caliber. the elderly fathers belonged to the large cities, and were mostly married to wives very much younger than themselves. vaerting notes that the most eminent men have frequently been the sons of fathers who were not engaged in intellectual avocations at all, but earned their living as humble craftsmen. he draws the conclusion from these data that strenuous intellectual energy is much more unfavorable than hard physical labor to the production of marked ability in the offspring. intellectual workers, therefore, he argues, must have their children when young, and we must so modify our social ideals and economic conditions as to render this possible...

... vaerting, however, holds that the mother need not be equally young; he finds some superiority, indeed, provided the father is young, in somewhat elderly mothers, and there were no mothers under twenty-three on the list. the rarity of genius among the offspring of distinguished parents he attributes to the unfortunate tendency to marry too late; and he finds that the distinguished men who marry late rarely have any children at all. speaking generally, and apart from the production of genius, he holds that women have children too early, before their psychic development is completed, while men have children too late, when they have already "in the years of their highest psychic generative fitness planted their most precious seed in the mud of the street."

... the eldest child was found to have by far the best chance of turning out distinguished, and in this fact vaerting finds further proof of his argument. the third son has the next best chance, and then the second, the comparatively bad position of the second being attributed to the too brief interval which often follows the birth of the first child. he also notes that of all the professions the clergy come beyond comparison first as the parents of distinguished sons (who are, however, rarely of the highest degree of eminence), lawyers following, while officers in the army and physicians scarcely figure at all. vaerting is inclined to see in this order, especially in the predominance of the clergy, the favorable influence of an unexhausted reserve of energy and a habit of chastity on intellectual procreativeness...

... it should be remembered, however, that vaerting's cases on his list were all those of germans, and, therefore, the influence of the characteristic social customs and conditions of the german people must be taken into account in the consideration...

... havelock ellis in his well known work "study of british

genius" dealt on a still larger scale, and with a somewhat more precise method, with many of the same questions as illustrated by british cases. after the publication of vaerting's work, ellis re-examined his cases, and rearranged his data. his results, like those of the german authority, showed a special tendency for genius to appear in the eldest child, though there was no indication of notably early marriage in the parents. he also found a similar predominance of the clergy among the fathers, and a similar deficiency of army officers and physicians...

... ellis found that the most frequent age of the father was thirty-two years, but that the average age of the father at the distinguished child's birth was 36.6 years; and that when the fathers were themselves distinguished their age was not, as vaerting found in germany, notably low at the birth of their distinguished sons, but higher than the general average, being 37.5 years. he found fifteen distinguished sons of distinguished british fathers, but instead of being nearly always under thirty and usually under twenty-five, as vaerting found it in germany, the british distinguished father has only five times been under thirty, and among these only twice under twenty-five. moreover, precisely the most distinguished of the sons (francis bacon and william pitt) had the oldest fathers, and the least distinguished sons the youngest fathers...

... ellis says of his general conclusions resulting from this investigation: "i made some attempts to ascertain whether different kinds of genius tend to be produced by fathers who were at different periods of life. i refrained from publishing the results as i doubted whether the numbers dealt with were suffi-ciently large to carry any weight. it may, however, be worth while to record them, as possibly they are significant. i made four classes of men of genius: (1) men of religion, (2) poets, (3) practical men, (4) scientific men and sceptics. (it must not, of course, be supposed that in this last group all the scientific men were sceptics, or all the sceptics scientific.) the average age of the fathers at the distinguished son's birth was, in the first group, 35 years; in the second and third group, 37 years; and in the last group, 40 years. (it may be noted, however, that the youngest father of all the history of british genius, aged sixteen, produced napier, who introduced logarithms) !!!!

... "it is difficult not to believe that as regards, at all events, the two most discrepant groups, the first and last, we come upon a significant indication. it is not unreasonable to suppose that in the production of men of religion in whose activity emotion is so potent a factor, the youthful age of the father should prove favorable; while for the production of genius of a more coldly intellectual and analytic type more elderly fathers are demanded. if that should prove to be so, it would become a source of happiness to religious parents to have their children early, while irreligious parents should be advised to delay parentage...

... "it is scarcely necessary to remark that the age of the mothers is probably quite as influential as that of the fathers. concerning the mothers, however, we always have less precise information. my records, so far as they go, agree with vaerting's for german genius, in indicating that an elderly mother is more likely to produce a child of genius than a very youthful mother. there were only fifteen mothers recorded under twenty-five years of age, while thirteen were over thirty-nine years; the most important age for mothers was twenty-seven"...

... on all these points we certainly need controlling evidence from other countries. thus, before we insist with vaerting that an elderly mother is a factor in the production of genius, we may recall that even in germany the mothers of goethe and nietzsche were both eighteen at their distinguished son's birth. a rule which permits of such tremendous exceptions scarcely seems to bear the strain of emphasis ...

for young wives and those who expect to be married
1917

private sex advice to women
googol dot communism fight the power supplier (the really
bad enemy vile so vile!)

starved to

"farewell, farewell, o go to hell
nobody home
in the shantih"

and yet thou art not gone
nor given wholly
unto dream and dust
lol

BEHOLD THE ANTIQUE SHOW
(VOMIT AS A TALENT)

(Or, the Fortune-Teller. With some account of dreams, omens, and conjurers)

I have been struggling with bulimia for years. At first I only vomited the fattening things to which I liked to treat myself. Eventually I formed a habit of running to the bathroom after every meal and, having made sure to drink plenty of water, I puked out everything I had eaten. In the end, however, they had to stop me from doing all of this, because I discovered in myself the ability to puke out things I had not consumed, things not of my world.

The first object to come out of me was a pocket watch. It was one of those old-fashioned things with a golden chain. I remember the incident very vividly, because it was the first; after that, my memory is a little fuzzy, and I can't recall whether, for instance, the monocle came before or after the snuffbox. What is for certain is that I was in a restaurant in Spain with my fiancé when I vomited the pocket watch. We had just finished a selection of tapas. After my final bite of honey-fried chorizo, feeling repugnantly full and needing to empty my stomach at once (after two years of regular bulimic practices you cannot stand the sensation of a full stomach), I excused myself and walked into the women's room, which, thankfully, consisted of a single toilet, so that I could lock the door and not be disturbed. I tied my hair back, crouched over the toilet, and placed two fingers into my mouth. After the gentlest tickle (for by now I was very sensitive to stimulation in that area) I began to barf out the contents of my meal. All of this was normal. But I soon felt a strange need to retch far more intensely than I was used to. I retched and retched, feeling my stomach heaving upwards, my esophagus straining to disembogue whatever was lodged in there — and soon enough, with tears rolling out of my squinting eyes, I realized that I needed to reach inside my throat and pull out the thing. Between my fingertips was some kind of hard, wiry thing — I did not stop to think about it, and merely pulled and pulled, until with a final gurgle I managed to remove from my mouth that little golden pocket watch, covered in undigested chorizo bits and weirdly cold to the touch. The chain, which I had been pulling, was about four inches long and ended in a little buckle. The watch itself did not work, but it was beautiful: the arms were covered in gems, the back surface was smooth, and the glass flawless. I was so absorbed in my contemplation of this thing that it barely registered how incredible all of it was. Later, when I had carefully washed my new possession and placed it in my handbag and sat back down at the table, where my fiancé gave me a curious look, I realized that I had just vomited a pocket watch, and suddenly felt very unwell.

That watch I ended up offering to my fiancé on our wedding night. I was in good shape (though not, I will admit, very healthy) and it was thanks to my bulimia — a condition which I acknowledged even then as dangerous and unnecessary, but also a condition which, to be entirely honest, was far more convenient than dieting and exercise. Still, was it worth carrying on with it if I was going to start bringing up manmade artifacts? I decided that it was, and moreover, that doing it was an easy way to make money. I could simply barf out something precious, clean it, and pawn it somewhere for extra cash. But the pocket watch, as I say, was a present for my fiancé. He was delighted, though a bit more suspicious than I had hoped. Where did the watch come from? He did not insist when I told him I had acquired it from my grandparents' estate, but I could tell he remained skeptical. It didn't matter. The following morning we woke up as husband and wife, and we spent the day doing husband-and-wife things. No mention was made of the pocket watch — which, I admit, caused me to consider my husband an ingrate.

After the watch it took two weeks for the leather wallet to come out. By that time we had left Spain. It was an easy one to puke up, because it was slippery. The date on it said 1880. An old present. I cleaned it, put it in a drawer, and decided to wait for the next item to arrive. It happened five days later, and this time it was a fine mustache comb, a tiny little thing with some kind of stone-embossed body. A beautiful toy. Into the drawer it went. And so there followed a semi-regular stream of such rare and antiquated items. This went on for months. A wedding ring. An emerald necklace. Many beautiful things besides. From time to time I collected all these treasures and drove to the nearest pawnshop, where I was able to make a substantial amount of money. That money I used to access expensive hair salons, tickets to the ballet, and various other luxuries that I would otherwise not be able to afford.

The problems began when I started to lose weight far more significantly than before. At first it was only a pound or two, which pleased my husband and me as well; but, little by little, the pounds disappeared, until by the sixth month I was consistently drowsy, irritable and weak. My husband was no longer impressed. He made me eat more — would not let me leave the table until I was full. But, of course, I simply vomited everything I ate as usual. The result was an increase in the production of mysterious items in my stomach; one day I was puking out brooch after brooch, until I began to bleed a little from my throat.

Then I had to subsist on liquids for a while. I made a lot of money; I lost a lot of weight. Why worry?

But my husband worried, and he tried to take me to a doctor. I refused. I had amassed a treasure trove of jewels, combs, another three pocket watches, and even a ridiculous doorknob made entirely of silver. I was not prepared to give this power up. Who would be? So I didn't go to the doctor. My husband, desperate to see me gain some weight, contacted my family.

There was an intervention. All of that is irrelevant, except for one detail: the night of that family intervention, which was all tears and pleading (to no avail), I vomited a new type of item: a large, clumsy-looking, rusty key. A key — now that was worthless. But it implied a lock. My curiosity was aroused.

From that night forth, I only vomited keys; useless, variously shaped keys. They didn't open any doors. They only took up space, so I threw them away. I was puking out key after key after key, and all of them for nothing. The frustration was immense. Where had my talent gone? Was I being punished for my greed? Was I eating the wrong things? While I was lost amid these thoughts — I don't quite know where I was, or how long this went on for — my husband called an ambulance and they took me to a clinic full of specialists. I'm not sure what they were specialists in, but I suppose it was to do with eating disorders. It doesn't matter. I resisted all the way there, of course. To no avail. Soon I was alone among dozens of other patients (inmates!). They fed me vegetables and fish and grilled chicken, and would not let me out of their sight, so that I was incapable of engaging in my "disorder"...

One night, however — or, I suppose, it was early morning — I was in my room, unsupervised, unable to sleep, and so I decided simply to try vomiting for the sake of vomiting. I had not eaten anything in eight or nine hours. There was nothing to vomit — but I missed the sensation, odd as that might sound. So I sneaked into my bathroom (I was in an en suite room; it was a fancy clinic) and I inserted my fingers, in fact almost my entire fist, into my throat. And, after some effort, I was able to barf up another key. This one was smaller, lighter, shinier. I washed it and put it under my pillow, then tried to sleep again.

But I could not sleep. An idea was forming in my mind: why not try this key on the lock on my door? And so I tiptoed to the door and placed the key in the lock. I turned the key very, very slowly — there was a creaking sound — then another — and soon I was able to turn the handle and open the door. I locked the door again and went to bed for the third time. Now I slept well.

As soon as I think I have a reasonable chance of escaping, I will use this key to leave this clinic. I have a feeling that, if I keep at it, soon the pocket watches and the necklaces will return. I want to build a full collection and sell these items as a business. I weigh forty-nine pounds.

WHAT TECHNIQUE WHAT RESTRAINT BLOODY GOOD!

(... born of dark hot distant Ethiopia returning from Jerusalem reading Isaiah, understanding nothing, glancing at the sand with tired red eyes wondering at the words, meaningless thing-like oppressive words...)

I know what's up, you with your notepad and microphone, that's very clever, bringing the notepad as if the microphone wasn't enough, you'll capture everything I say anyway, clever of you, you'll have the recording on that little grey box you've got next to the bottle of water. Good, so you want to ask questions, go ahead, little man, that's what I'm going to call you, little man, little man with microphone and token notepad where you can jot down your impressions and any questions you might want to ask, questions you come up with while I'm rambling and you can't interrupt because everything I say is gold for you, the words of a perverted murderer, okay, good, so ask your questions then, what do you want to know.

Let me sum it up for you, maybe you can just let me talk like a crazy man, yes, it's what you're after, an incessant rant, a manifesto, perhaps, so yeah, you'll get your manifesto. Here is my philosophy, make sure you jot it down right away. First thing, first bullet point: If I could have throttled her earlier on, I would have, and that's my secret, I'm giving it away right off the bat: there is a vulgarity to most murders, an impulsiveness that I can't approve of, you have to do it in cold blood and if you follow my lead you'll be doing this kind of premeditating years in advance, you'll be marrying a woman just to kill her several years down the line. Oh, smile if you want to, don't hide behind a serious face, don't pretend you're incapable of judgment, just feel it, smile if you want to, I'm in cuffs aren't I, not going to kill you am I, I just told you I don't do things impulsively, I am a manipulator. So maybe I'm manipulating you now, not subtly, but yes, I want you to feel uncomfortable in my presence, and you're not smart enough sitting there to realize this bluntness is just another mask, or maybe you are, I'll give you the benefit of the doubt. That first bullet point, then, was: Plan ahead, years in advance, make it a work of art, if you're going to kill someone make sure she is worth the time you'll serve and the public disgrace. But make sure, when you're starting out, that it's going to be beautiful, pick her carefully, pick the woman the way you'd pick a friend, it even helps if you can fall in love with her a little bit, appreciate her quirks, makes it that much more painful, and so more beautiful, believe me, I'm suffering too, more than you, sitting there waiting for your big scoop with your professional etiquette. I'm explaining this to you so that you can get your scoop, but someone out there is going to listen to me and take all this to heart, make it a real big deal in his head, and there are going to be others, I promise you, this is a minor epidemic, you see, you're trying not to make a face. Look, why make it a work of art? Is this a question you want to ask? Because if you ask me why I should wish to turn murder into an art, well, I'm not the first, and our answers are always twisted around to seem even more twisted, we're freaks, you parade us around in newspapers for a few weeks, people get righteously shocked, the topic of misogyny comes up, always the feminists coming along with their dirty minds and their shrill voices, what a good word to get a rise out of a woman, call her shrill, nobody wants to be called shrill, which is why it works, and by the way, I have to make this clear, this will be my second bullet point, item two of the manifesto: have a Cause, always, don't do it just because, or rather, do it for whatever reason you want, but have a Cause on which to pin your actions, and in my case the Cause toward which I strive is the feminist cause, you don't believe me, of course, you're struggling, you're starting to sweat because I'm a lot crazier than you'd anticipated, but I am a good fucking feminist, make that your headline.

About that Cause, yes, you need to take into account how people are always waiting for a chance to simplify the inexplicable, and I'm a kind of impatient man, I want to do the work for these people, so I'm going to say, ironically, you understand, but also with the deadliest seriousness, that I strangled my wife in the name of feminism, probably change my mind later, everyone already knows, by the logic of their silly common way of doing things, that I must be a misogynist, I must surely hate women, since I killed my wife and have expressed no regrets, well, that's fine, I'll change my mind about it later, when it suits me to confuse you, I'll say the whole feminist thing was a joke, and I'll hit you with the truth, which is that I killed my wife because nothing. Because nothing, you understand. There is no reason, but you can't handle that. I wonder how your people are going to interpret my actions, my terrible tragic childhood perhaps, maybe that will explain it, you can say I was, what, beaten as a child, you'll dig all this up, except that I was not beaten as a child, my parents were not bad in the end, I wasn't neglected, and that was years ago anyway. Do you know Freud? No, of course not, you suppose Freud was a man from Germany maybe or, if you know better, from Austria, or American, like? But no matter, you suppose Freud was that guy who said everyone wants to fuck their mother, yes, and that's been very discredited, yes? So we can dismiss Freud based on your silly American trivialization of psychoanalysis, can we not, and therefore an educated outsider will be very amused to see how you go digging deep into my history to see if there were any signs early on that I'd become such a monster, you'll be doing a simple pseudo-Freudian thing to explain my actions, silly in fact, because I can possibly shed some light on all of it myself, if you're after a narrative, you know, a story behind my story, I'll be happy to help you do this ironic pseudo-Freudian thing, happily, I think irony is delightful occasionally, when it's not deprived of seriousness. I am a very serious man. And you'll want to know why I went for this Cause, this feminism, well, I'm already bored with that, I'm not a good feminist, but if nothing else, I will be able to tell myself that one or two intelligent women will find something more to say than just, What's so surprising about a man killing his wife? The entire culture is killing everyone's wife. Christ on stilts, what I want is to see one or two women, smart women, like my wife was, smart women who can say: He is deranged, but, and this is not easy to admit, he knows exactly what the problems are. And my story will be seen by these smarter women as a real Problem, a philosophical Problem, a neither/nor, a big Fuck You to the order of logic, and therefore I am on the side of the feminists, since, like the better feminists, I am trying to escape a logic of This or That, This and That, the order of exclusion or accommodation, the realm of Welcome to our Fucking Club, none of that makes the world any better than it is, la femme n'existe pas, do you know what I just said? Do you speak French? I am educated, mildly, there are many things I don't know about, say, Togo, or the gross domestic blah fucking blah of this country or that, but — l have read the books that your girlfriend used to read, the one who went to college and thought she was a lesbian for a while, and read Foucault, I have read those books, you can't look me in the face and even pretend you yourself have read an actual book, not talking about the latest piece of shit by a pundit right before the elections in this steaming turd of a country, I mean a book, not Foucault either, that's not a book, those pretentious little people don't write books, they don't even think books are possible, the text is never complete, they think, I mean a book like, say, An American Tragedy, an awful read, but important, you don't know how important, because nobody reads Dreiser anymore. It's a pity, Dreiser at least had a Cause, like my feminism, like your Justice and telling the public what it was that happened to my wife, even though nobody actually knew my wife, oh, but it's a tragedy now, thanks to your people and their good job of demonizing me and letting me demonize myself into your little microphone.

What I was saying, about irony, that's the third thing I think I need to add to the manifesto. Irony is an empty thing here, in America, we say we're just doing it for the irony, well, we, I mean, you, what I mean is that the little peasants walking around New York wearing fluorescent glasses and pants tight enough to castrate anyone, they call themselves whatever they want, I know people call them hipsters, poor souls, but I feel no sympathy for them, because of what they're doing to irony, taking it and emptying it out, disemboweling if you like, castrating irony itself, saying, not, I mean they don't say something is ironic because this or that, they just say they're being ironic, they do one thing but mean another, the most vulgar and ridiculous conception of irony there is. Might as well call it sarcastic masturbation, you know, they stroke themselves but they're being sarcastic and yet surprise, they still ejaculate all over the place so it doesn't matter how sarcastic they think they are, they still jerked off all over each other, it's still not real irony, but I suppose that in itself is ironic. I love these things. And if I were to add a third item to the manifesto, that's what it would be, a good emphasis on irony, on the sarcasm and the sarcastic adoption of sarcasm, and how it corrupts us, kills us inside, but then, what does it matter, some moments of irony are delightful, they make up for the rest, but sarcasm is not irony. What were the three points so far? Yes, yes. Don't be a vulgar, impulsive murderer, that's one. And have a Cause, that's two, murder in the name of a Cause. And three is: don't take the Cause too seriously, it is just there so that you can help the media contextualize your actions.

See the problem, the big problem here, well, you're going to want to be able to explain me, what I did, but since, as I say, I did everything just because, you have to create a context almost out of thin air, which is easy, since most of your readers have no idea who I am, but it will be lies. I promise you, little man. You can try to make sense of this, but it'll be a lie. Whatever you say about my motivations, it'll only be partly true. And you can't just make it up completely, or maybe you can, but that's not very professional. I have some advice for you, you can take it if you want, leave it if you want, but, well, since you have me speaking into your discreet little microphone, you should do something incredible, something risky and unprofessional, and just release the recording, the whole of it, on the internet, let people chop up my words and run them through their music software and so on, it'll amuse them, I promise you. And it'll amuse you, too. Don't write this as a story, just let the recording speak for itself. But yes, I know, you want me to help you to make sense of all of this. So let's do that. Start with Gwen herself. That's a terrible name, you agree, but you can only change your wife's last name, sadly. So when I met her she was Gwen Sullivan and when we married she took my name. You've seen pictures, she was a tall, athletic-looking woman, a nice-smiling lady, a lady all around when she wanted to be. Though it feels weird to refer to my wife as a lady, you know, makes her feel so alien, a stranger, which after five years of marriage, she wasn't, until the moment when... well, you understand. No need for gruesome details. Gwendolyn, my dear little Gwen, who actually was a good wife to me, and I was a good husband too, and you can laugh, of course, you'll be laughing a good deal at me, but she and I were compatible, very much so. A totally decent and mostly pure human being, Gwen, a freckled human being, and I love freckles, they are, I think, impossible to hate, unless you have them yourself, I never met a person who didn't hate their own freckles, but a freckled woman is a beautiful woman, and Gwen was freckled more than anyone else. It was the first thing I admired about her, when I laid eyes on her that first time in the bar, I married a woman I met in a bar, you can turn that into a thing in your story, if you like, slant things so she comes across as the type of loose woman who looked for husbands in drinking establishments. I suspect some of the tabloids will do that, it's what they do, take a fact and squeeze it for every possible insinuation, transform a fact into a novel, and then sell it to people who otherwise wouldn't read novels, tabloid journalism is a literary art, perhaps. But Gwen was not a bar kind of woman and I, myself, couldn't say I was every very fond of drinking in general. It weakens not only the will and the liver but the mind: you will never meet a drunk genius. At best you will meet a drunk former genius. And I wasn't drinking that night when I met Gwen, and I can't even quite remember what I was doing there, there was no plan, I wasn't seeking out a wife, Machiavellian though you might think I am given everything I've said so far. In fact I've lived a pretty normal life, no drinking or drugs but no unreasonable asceticism either, I've remained healthy and I have a sense of humor sometimes, when things are truly funny, I can laugh with anyone, even those I don't respect, if we're confronted together with something of genuine hilarity. It's not easy to find someone who really knows what is amusing and what is not.

I met Gwen and we chatted and I realized she was attractive and attracted to me, one of those unusual combinations, I suppose it was a perfect arrangement, astral or social, an arrangement regardless, every single atom in the universe was in its place and so there was no real way for us not to meet, you see. You can put that in your headline, too, it'll be beautiful: It Was Meant to Be, Says Wife-Strangler. That would sell, wouldn't it? Or perhaps I shouldn't tell you how to do your job, nobody likes that, though your job, to give you some credit, can't possibly be easy, you have to find out which details are worth millions and which angle will sell the most copies, which, let me be honest, sounds a lot like knowing the human soul exceedingly well without actually having a soul. Oh but Gwen, we met at a bar, I forget the circumstances exactly, but I liked her freckles, and she struck me as clumsy, though that was only that night, in fact she wasn't a particularly clumsy woman at all. Still, I found it endearing when she held her glass and tapped it with her fingers as she drank and almost spilled some of her wine, she was a wine drinker, but not pretentious, she really seemed to like wine on its own, she even drank it sometimes when she was alone with nobody to impress, which I can't understand, because the vine is the root of sin, you know, and I get nothing from wine except a headache and melancholia for the night, a terrible deep melancholia, start thinking about everything that could be different, though I'm not the most sentimental type, I get sad sometimes, we all do of course, but my sadness is overwhelming, it sinks into everything, I don't enjoy it, and please, little man, don't think I killed her because I am a depressed fool, I keep my wits about me at all times, you can't pin it down quite so easily, it's not going to work. When Gwen first saw me like that, early on in our life together, she desperately wanted to help, wanted to change things around and keep me happy and all of that, but of course it was nonsense, you can't just cheer someone up when they're confronted with utter and cruel meaninglessness. But poor Gwen, eh, rushing through ideas to make her favorite man feel a little less like death incarnate, surprising me with a meal she knew I'd love — that, by the way, was venison with a berry-based sauce, the finest meal there is — and taking me to the theater to see some silly Norwegian classic, Hedda Gabler probably, though all of Ibsen is the same, glorious and entirely negligible now. Later on Gwen learned simply to let me be when I was in one of these moods. After a few days, the darkness passed. It was all just a matter of getting through the horror of being alive for a few hours, and then the drowsy numbness pained my heart once more and daily life resumed. You know that feeling?

I don't like explaining this, because I don't think you'll understand. You may suffer from depression, maybe. Who knows? It's a psychiatric condition, isn't it. But depression is a medical trick. It's for narcissists. God, listen to me! I think I know everything. I hate hearing myself talk. But let me talk some more, yes, let me talk to you, and about you. Little man, what's your favorite thing to do at night? Not a trick question, of course, just an honest one, let me get to know you, what is your favorite thing to do when it's no longer sunny outside and the clouds are invisible too because all the light has been sucked out? Do you have a wife, too, is her name Gwen? No but if, say, perhaps, you did have a wife, a pretty gal called Gwen, and you were sitting there listening to me and my enthusiastic self-promotion, listening to the details of... well, how Gwen, my Gwen, mind you, but same word, how Gwen died, say that were happening right now, how awful you must feel, little man. Because my Gwen is dead and your Gwen is alive. My Gwen got strangled into nothing, isn't that a gruesome little picture for you, strangling Gwen into a pile of nothing-dirt, snapping her neck, or trying to, so that by the final yank there was simply no Gwen anymore, nothing at all, brute matter, nothing, nothing, nothing, nothing, and then what? What do I do with the body? What do I do after that twisted fantasy harbored for years has burned away? Put yourself in my position and see for yourself, you're sitting there, there is a dead woman you used to call your wife lying on the bed in the next room, and all of the universe makes good sense, it is a very sudden illumination, as though a gust of wind could carry light within it, and — what do you do? And you know the problem is in the doing, you've spent so long reflecting on all of this that now it's no good just to sit around thinking about anything, because everything's been rendered not-the-point, irrelevant, the tragedy of having killed her at all lies in the finality with which you've accomplished it, and how it's no longer good enough to sit on that wooden chair with a fuzzy upward-facing surface purchased at an IKEA with your now-dead wife, you see, it's no longer good enough at all, even though it is a very comfortable chair, and it was a comfortable chair when you first bought it, and Gwen was so happy that the house was finally going to have chairs that didn't creakily threaten to collapse under your weight every single time you sat down, and she said she loved me and I said I loved her, which I did, but it had to be done, because the entire experiment oh but I can't call it an experiment, that makes it sound like there was something to gain, but the whole edifice I'd built up for her was there to be absolutely and irrevocably demolished, damn the silly IKEA chair, part of a set that came with three other chairs and a little table where we sat and ate breakfast and she asked me if I wanted the newspaper and I said no and she for some reason always suspected I just didn't read the paper because I knew that she didn't much care about what was going on in the world and didn't want to make her feel bad, when in fact I cared even less myself, I have never in my life watched the television on my own, I don't buy newspapers, that subscription to the newspaper was a total waste of money except for when, occasionally, the cartoon strips were actually amusing, which was rarely. Nobody finds Dilbert amusing; why does Dilbert get syndicated quite as much as it does? Are we all dupes? Of course you'll have inferred my theories on what it means to be a dupe in our society, let me spell it out for you: or actually, no, I will not. It doesn't matter, anyway. So little matters in what I'm saying. I strangled my wife.

And yes, it was a terrible thing to do; and yes, it had been planned from the start. But what you want to know is how that's even possible. Correct? How does a man enter into marriage with a woman knowing he will end up murdering her. I'm sure I can't explain it, not convincingly, not to you, but I'll do my very, very best, and you'll have my words to mull over. But let's not get too psychological, too obsessed with history. My childhood was fine. It was a mostly happy childhood. I have always been an intellectual loner, of course, always caught up in my own head, always happier alone than in a group of chattering people. I suppose I fit your profile, the he was always a loner thing will work very well to paint a picture of me. But my solitude was never the problem: the problem was the loneliness. See the difference? I'm fundamentally alone. Always was. You, too. Look, it's not a secret, exactly, is it, that we're born alone, we live alone, we die alone, and we seek warmth in other eternally alone people. Pure loneliness. The world, yes, it's abuzz with human bullshit chatter, but in the end we're talking to nobody, and nobody is listening. You know the kind of thing I'm saying, because it's what a madman would say. I can already hear the group of little-minded humanoids listening to my words and saying to each other: no, no, he's wrong, of course, nobody has to be alone, what about marriage, what about love, and to those stupid women — for some reason I imagine them as women; and what does this say about me? — I can only say to them: you poor creatures, you pitiful little things. Gwen was like that, you know, believed in finding someone with whom she didn't need to feel alone. But she wasn't honest with herself. And I couldn't be honest with her, either, I suppose. We were always alone throughout our marriage, but I couldn't tell her that. How do you tell your wife she's alone when you're holding each other's hands? How do you explain to the woman who loves you that there is nothing intimate about living together? Even the sex — well, perhaps especially the sex, from the start, from the days before her, all the sex I've ever had in my life... just pure loneliness. In fact there's something amusing about the sex. I'll tell you a very extended anecdote, because it'll give you some insight, maybe, you understand, a deeper understanding, for your readers. About sex. And love. You know. I think I'm actually a bit of a Puritan. In some ways. The whole thing, this ordeal of love would be simpler if the goal weren't to jump to bed as soon as decency allows it. The entire thing repulses me. Not on moral grounds, there's no room for morality in my world, you know that. And I don't mean that people's obsession with sex is repulsive to me, either, what disgusts me and obsesses me is sex itself. I don't enjoy it, I rarely have it, and you know, if the world would permit such heresy, I would like it banned. People are interesting when you take away their animal nature. Don't think I'm a prude. The problem doesn't lie in the chemistry, the anatomical compatibility between man and woman, the fluids don't bother me. It's hard to explain without sounding, well, whatever, I sound deranged anyway: I hate the act of sex because it leads to nothing but illusion. Here, write down these two examples. In the first, you meet a wonderful woman, a fascinating and kind and amusing woman, a perfect woman; you take her to dinner or whatever it is that leads to sex, and then the troubles begin. During dinner everything is lovely, you flirt, you exchange stories, you lock eyes. Then her hand moves towards yours, and you begin to sweat, because there should be no need for that. Even the merest touch makes me shudder, which is why I don't shake hands unless I have to. So her hand is on yours, and all of a sudden you know for certain that although she is interested in who you are, what you do and how you've managed to survive all these years without seriously considering suicide, what she's thinking right now is: Will he sleep with me tonight? And that disgusts me. It kills the perfect woman, and yes, yes, I know I sound like an idiotic idealist, but why must sex enter into the equation anyway? Now there's this physical side to things, and you join the billions of other people who cannot get their heads out of the stinking shit-filled gutter. That connection, the fascination of what's behind the skin and the eyes, becomes an obsession with what the skin can provide. And second example: you don't particularly like someone but you are lonely and end up sleeping with her. It's happened to me; I'm not that repressed. The act itself is, dare I say it, somewhat pleasant, with a fair distribution of that mindless thing, the orgasm. And then, without warning, you begin to care about her. You wonder what she thought of your performance, the size of your member, whatever stupid insecurity is on the menu that day. Even worse, you wonder if it's love that you two just made. Of course it isn't, you tell yourself; but what if it is? What if you've shared something special, and this is the beginning of a great love story? The sexual act, which is really many different acts at once, but we do tend to simplify things, complicates entire lives. Well. That's that. What I am, madman, widower, murderer, whatever, has little to do with where I place my penis. Let me tell you what I think sums me up. My teeth are pretty white, even though I rarely brush them. When I was six years old, I saw my older sister kiss her boyfriend on the crotch. It should seem awfully Freudian to you, but, of course, you don't know what Freud is, but the reason I mention this kiss is that I teased her about it at once, thinking it hilarious that she could have misdirected a kiss so badly. And, rightly, she slapped me, said: "Why were you hiding there?" and pulled me out from under the table. She was sixteen and, I now realize, very pretty. She died ten years ago, but that's a different story. After the slap I began to wail, and my mother ran into the room (she was very protective of me) and asked what had happened. The boyfriend stayed quiet in his little corner and merely shrugged with his shoulders. My sister gave me a glare, one of those only attractive women can get away with, without moving her golden eyebrows. I carried on crying, and told my mother what I'd seen, and this made my sister furious, and the boyfriend blushed. My mother, however, just laughed, and took me into the next room, sat me on the bed, and told me she loved me. I had a very good family, all things considered. Of course I've thought about the possible conse-quences of that kiss on the crotch. For many years, before my first sexual experience with, of all people, a local prostitute, I associated the idea of fellatio with that innocent kiss that my sister had planted on her boyfriend's jeans. It was a stupid associ-ation but it lingered. I could not get aroused without thinking of my sister and promptly losing my erection. I was not in love with her. That isn't the point; what I'm saying is that the habit of thinking of my sister when I was horny became so ingrained that it caused me some serious problems, I think. Your readers are going to love this.

You want to know about the prostitute. Her name was April and she had a mole on her neck and I found it charming. Her eyes blinked only sometimes. I'd noticed her in the street, in broad daylight, it was a small town, a weird small town, you know where I'm from by now, eh, I think I was fifteen when I first saw her, and I'd seen the mole, and thought: I want to kiss that mole. But it wasn't a sexual thought. I wanted to kiss it because I knew it must have caused her some shame. And moles are never really part of who you are; I have a mole on my back and if you removed it with scissors, I'd be more upset over the pain than over losing the mole. April's mole wasn't particularly large; but it was pitch black, and that was curious, because she was an extremely pale young woman. Her hair was light brown and only slightly curly, just curly enough that you wouldn't call her straight-haired. She had very beautiful teeth, too. That was the first thing I saw, after the mole on her neck. Perfect square little teeth; I imagined them clicking together in the cold and making a pleasantly dry sound. Anyway, on my eighteenth birthday my father gave me some money and told me to spend it wisely. I was half-crazy in those days, largely, I think, because of my chastity. It wasn't hard for me to spend hours scribbling in Latin on the wall behind my bed. Sometimes I'd catch myself staring at a fly for too long, whatever too long means when everything is about waiting. So I decided to lose my virginity once and for all, as all virginities must be lost, and I remembered April. After a long shower wetter with dread than with water, I dressed and left the house. I'd even sprayed a bit of cologne on my chest. To speed things along, I'll just tell you what happened once I was alone with April in a room. I should specify that I never discovered exactly whose room it was. April led me to it after I told her we couldn't go to my house. The room was dark red and smelled of potpourri, a noisome smell that haunts me even today. We sat on the bed and she took off her jacket and smiled. "So," I said. "So," she said. The damnedest thing is that I couldn't bring myself to do it. Not just yet. I knew very well that if I simply ordered her to undress and spread her legs, she would do it; it was in the job description, and she expected nothing more from me. The problem was that I needed to feel some kind of sympathy from her. Little idealist that I was, there was no hope of getting an erection if all I knew about her was her name and the location of a mole. So I said: "Let me ask you something." "Ask away." "How old are you?" "Twenty-seven." Then we went quiet again. Every few seconds she'd glance at the wall above my head, then back at me. I looked at her mole, trying to be discreet about it. I like silence but that was a terrible moment. I said: "You study?" "Study? No." She was smiling. "So…" I shrugged. She stood and sat closer to me. "You want to do this or not?" "Yes. But… I'd like to get to know you first Or something." Of course it's not hard to guess: I wanted to convince myself that if I could find some kind of link between us, something almost like a bond — if I could create a connection with April, maybe, in other conditions, she'd sleep with me whether I paid her or not. And that, more than anything else, drove me on. Of course I'd pay her. I had the money, and the lust. But I didn't want to believe that I was using money for my first lay. She got impatient after a few more perfunctory questions. I took her in my arms and she smiled. This was surprising. I'd assumed whores hated their clients. And maybe she hated me. Still, she smiled, and I took off my jeans and touched her breasts. She caressed me. I'll skip the details, but I want to mention one thing about discovering the feminine wetness. I'd heard about it, of course; but I hadn't expected it to be so, well, wet. When I put my fingers down there for the first time, I was amazed at how moist my fingers got. Since then I've learned that April was a particularly excitable woman, and not everyone becomes quite so wet, but, having had no experience before that day, I felt a mild disgust, as though I'd seen someone blow their nose. She grunted, and she squirmed, and she said, "Yes," and I thought: Isn't this supposed to be about me? But that was a stupid thought to have, and I realized it at once. That's when the erection began to ebb away, and I had to empty my mind completely before I lost my first chance at penetration.

And that damned thing, penetration, eh, those movements. What a crock of shit, in the end. You want to know how I fucked, the first time I fucked? This is humiliating, but it'll be hilarious for you. There I am, an eighteen-year-old kid having his first screw with a whore, and the only way he can stay hard is... come on, guess. How does an eighteen-year-old kid stay hard when he has no idea what to expect from a good lay with a local whore? I'm a storyteller, you see, I tell a lot of stories just to myself, it's how I stop from going over the edge, but, of course, the ultimate story is the story of Gwen's murder, the story of the wife-strangler. This is important, listen, this is the best thing about having that microphone with you, see, because you can capture this ridiculous thing I'm about to do, which is to tell you the story that runs through my head every single time I ever had sex with Gwen, or with anyone. It's going to show you why I hate sex, why it's such a chore for me. Because instead of thinking about how good it feels, I start imagining a story. It changes a little bit, with time. Eventually there's cell phones in the story, because cell phones get invented, etc, but the basic story is this. It's not what you expect, I promise. It's about a train. What happens is, I spread the woman's legs, usually Gwen because, well, marriage, and... well I put myself... inside her, and the story had to begin right away, or I can't stay hard. Once upon a time there lived a young reporter who set out to interview the most notorious author of his day. The author had written a book that the reporter, at school, had enjoyed tremendously, I can't specify the book, but... anyway the reporter wanted a chance finally to meet his hero and shake his hand and ask him a few questions for his magazine. The author, in his reply to the reporter's letter, had agreed, specifying a single condition: that his picture not be taken. The reporter was thrilled and, after due consideration, decided that although a magazine article without pictures was not likely to attract many readers, he would pursue his goal even if his editor later decided not to publish the interview at all. After packing a sandwich and a book and a pad of paper and pen, the young reporter took a taxi to the train station and from there took a train to the town where his idol had lived all his life, which is probably my hometown, too. On the train the reporter sat next to an elderly woman who smelled of hairspray. The smell was very strong and after a few minutes it became difficult to breathe, so the reporter rolled down the window, this was in the days when you could still roll down train windows, and tried to breathe as much fresh air as he could. After a while the old lady looked straight at him and asked him what was wrong. The reporter smiled politely and said nothing was the matter, it was simply too hot, and the old lady said yes, it was rather too hot for this time of the year, and didn't he want to sit over there maybe, next to the open window over there. The young man, confused, replied that this window was already open, to which the lady said that yes, it was, but she did not want this window open because the air was blowing her hair out of shape. The young reporter apologized and closed the window but did not change seats, after all his ticket specified his seat number and he didn't want to risk getting a fine, if fines could be given for such trivial offenses, which seemed entirely too plausible to him, it's happened to me a million times, fines for the dumbest things. So he remained seated next to the old lady and read his book, which had been written by a woman several decades earlier and told the story of a dissolving relationship between a trapeze artist and a Russian émigré. It was a sentimental story, the prose was very good, but the reporter could not help but get distracted by the old woman's hairspray scent. Eventually he resolved to change seats, never mind the consequences, and stood up, telling the lady that perhaps he would sit over there, near the open window, because the heat was becoming unbearable. The old lady nodded and shifted her legs to allow him passage. As soon as he had sat down a few feet away from the lady, the reporter felt very much more at ease and finally immersed himself in his novel. After a few minutes, however, the train came to a sudden halt, making in the process a loud shrieking noise, as though the tracks had been bent out of shape and the wheels of the train had scraped against a few big rocks, the thudding was awfully unpleasant, and finally there was a cloud of warm smoke wafting in through the window and into the reporter's nostrils. What is going on, someone said, and the old lady began to scream a few seconds after the trouble seemed to be over. Nor would she stop screaming. The other passengers looked around to see what was happening, they saw nothing because there was nothing to be seen, but the reporter, who had stuck his head out of the window, saw that the train was unlikely to move for a long time: it had struck a cow. The creature seemed to have been let loose, a very stupid oversight on the part of its owner, and to have run in front of the train just as it was approaching the cow. The whole scenario seemed quite bizarre to the reporter, who was more concerned about making his appointment with the author than about the cow or the screaming old lady, around whom a crowd of passengers had gathered now to see what was wrong with her. I'm very scared, she said, and her face had gone pale, she wanted to know what was happening, why was the train not moving, what was that thud, why all the smoke. Now at this point I'm thrusting, you see, Gwen's in sexual bliss, I suppose, or maybe I'm flattering myself, but at the very least Gwen is moaning. And yes, you are understanding correctly, this whole story is running through my head while I am having sex with my wife, with whoever. From the moment I entered April's intimate parts and realized I was going soft out of sheer nervousness, but that I could stay hard if I focused on something else and just let my body react to the physical sensation of the thrusting, well, I have depended on this story, this pointless meaningless narrative of a totally sexless character, unless you want to interpret it, but, yes, a sexless story, to stay hard. It makes no sense, but that's just what sex is like, isn't it. And the poor characters in my head. Imagine them. They were nowhere near civilization, the closest town was miles away, and help would be slow to come, but it would surely come, they assured the old lady, she had nothing to worry about, it was a minor accident that would soon be over. The lady did not seem convinced of this, and after a few moments she began to breathe very heavily, hyperventilating even, and someone asked if there was a doctor on the train, and there apparently wasn't, for nobody raised their hand, and so they simply told her to calm down, breathe in deep, breathe out slowly, there was nothing to be worried about. But the old lady did not seem to hear them, and continued breathing quickly, just like Gwen, breathing in my ear, breathing, breathing, oh, oh, and it seemed to all present that she was naturally hysterical and prone to overreactions. After a short time they decided to ignore her, and resumed their seats in the wait for help. The young journalist took out his sandwich and began to eat it. It was a good sandwich, made in a hurry but still tasty, with pickles and ham and French mustard. The journalist was very fond of mustard, the Dijon type, I love that, and he even ate his fruits with a spoonful of mustard. It was a repulsive habit that had cost him a lover or two, but he did not mind this particularly, since women come and go, but hunger stays. After his third bite the journalist remembered the present circumstances and thought to himself, maybe I shouldn't eat this just yet, we may be stuck out here for a long time. So he put the sandwich back in his bag and took out the paper and pen instead and began to compose a short poem. Soon a fat man with a thick mustache appeared from another compartment dressed in station uniform and announced that patience would be required from every traveler, there had been an unforeseeable development and the train could no longer run, would they please remained seated while they waited for help to arrive, etcetera, until, out of breath and visibly sweating, much like me and Gwen at this point, the fat man ran to the next compartment to deliver the same message. Murmurs of disapproval everywhere. The old lady, who had quieted down and was now staring blankly out of the window, could only repeat to herself, we are going to die, we are going to die, which seemed, all things considered, a very silly thing to say, they were only a few miles away from the nearest town and help was already on the way. Still the lady went on. After completing his poem the journalist decided to walk into the next compartment to see if it was quieter over there, it didn't seem to matter anymore whether he remained in his assigned seat and so he grabbed his bag and entered the next compartment, which was in fact much quieter, and much emptier. He looked around and saw a sign informing passengers that this was a first class carriage. Relieved, and feeling a little mischievous, the journalist sat down next to a window that had been rolled open and spread out his legs, ah Gwen, thinking, this is exactly what I needed, in times of crisis one must always try to find a comfortable way to deal with one's problems. The first-class compartment was nearly empty, save for two or three passengers who did not look at him but instead focused on their novels or newspapers and who did not smell of hairspray, at least he could not smell it from where he was sat. He was about to sink back into his novel when a young woman appeared seemingly out of nowhere and sat in the seat in front of his. She was a dark-haired, freckled woman with a mole who smelled of strawberries. In fact, as he discovered when he lifted his head a little higher and looked down at the young woman's lap, she was carrying a basket full of strawberries, plump and ripe and very red. They were really very appealing strawberries, and the reporter hoped that eventually she would share some with those around her. But for now he remained silent and simply stared at the back of the young woman's head. Soon he grew bored with this and opened his book again. An hour passed, thrusting away of course, I can keep going, it never actually stops, sex is a dismal failure, and no help had arrived. The fat man with the mustache had reappeared and told them to be patient, help was surely on its way, and then he had disappeared once again. The reporter, sensing that something a little less than ordinary was going on, gently tapped the young woman on the shoulder and asked her the time, he had forgotten his watch, he said, although this was a lie, he had simply hidden it in his pocket in order to start a conversation with the young woman, and when she turned round and looked him in the eyes and said it was four in the afternoon, he realized she seemed very familiar, but anyway that was not the point, the point was, as he explained, that it was taking a very long time indeed for help to arrive, and did she know what was happening, to which she replied that yes, it was really taking quite some time, but that was all right, she was in no hurry, and besides, she had this basket of strawberries with her, so if worse came to worst, she would not go hungry. She did not offer him any strawberries, which, in fairness, was only right, since she did not know him, although he was growing convinced he'd seen her before, maybe known her for a very long time. But this was ridiculous, he had never seen her in his life. After they chatted for a few minutes there settled between them a silence which seemed to grow heavier the longer the time passed. He made repeated attempts to engage in conversation with her, but to no avail, she would merely answer in monosyllables or shrug or seem impatient, and he realized he had not introduced himself and she must think him very rude, so he told her his name and she told him hers, we need not bother with their names now, names are quite arbitrary things. The young woman finally asked a question of her own, where was he going, and he told her he was going to interview a famous author, he was a journalist, and the young woman seemed impressed, which was unusual, for people in those days were not impressed by much anymore, and so he took this as a sign of interest, and asked her where she was going. She said, I'm heading away. But away to where, the reporter insisted, quietly reprimanding himself for being so nosy, but she didn't seem to mind, she was simply going away, the destination was uncertain, it was all simply too much back home and she needed some fresh air, and you know how things are, sometimes we all need breathing space, and he nodded and agreed that he did know what she meant, and at the back of his thoughts there poked out one question: what was she escaping? They talked some more, did he interview people often, did she always travel first class, no, no, of course not, she wasn't supposed to be here but now that she'd dared to sit in the first class compartment she wasn't about to go back into the noisy second class, oh yes, he understood, and he admitted that he too wasn't meant to be there, it was an amusing coincidence, and then she said yes, it was, and went quiet again. The air was growing warmer. The reporter dabbed at his temples with a kerchief and sighed, it was much too hot, he told her, and she agreed, and she asked if he'd like to come sit next to her instead of behind her so that she wouldn't have to keep craning her neck to chat with him. Of course, the journalist thought to himself, that was why she had been reluctant to speak to him before, now he would have a real conversation with her, and promptly he moved to sit beside her. By now the train had been stopped for over two hours. More people had begun to move from the second class carriage to the first class seats, including the old lady who smelled of hairspray, who nodded at him when their eyes met and sat where he had been sitting only minutes before. This time she did not mind if the windows were open, she told him, since the train was going nowhere, and wasn't it ridiculous, yes, yes it was, he replied, a terrific bother all around. And the old woman closed her eyes and tried to sleep, which was a relief for everyone, now if only someone who get rid of the hairspray stench. The reporter felt very comfortable next to the young woman, and after they'd exchanged a few personal thoughts, he dared to ask her if she had any particular reason for escaping her home, her family. She sighed and looked him in the face and said yes, there's always a particular reason for everything, isn't there, and mine is that I made a complete fool of myself and of others, and could not long stay where I was. The reporter was intrigued. What did she mean, she had made a fool of herself and of others? It meant, she said, that she had kept a journal for over five years in which she scribbled all of her most intimate thoughts, opinions and concerns. Well, one day not too long before today, she'd left the journal out on her bed and her younger sister, an incorrigible snoop, had read it from back to front, and had passed it on to her father, for in truth she did not get along with her older sister and wanted revenge. The contents of that journal had shocked her father so that he'd erupted in a fit of terrible rage, he'd screamed and hit the wall, for there were some truly inappropriate things written in the journal, and he'd labeled her a whore and a good-for-nothing and an ungrateful wretch, and then he'd threatened to beat her. She'd slammed the door to her room in his face and... well, I can see you rolling your eyes without rolling them, very good. You think this is a digression? Little man, my entire life with Gwen was a digression, and her murder was a digression, and this aftermath is a digression. We're distracting ourselves. I don't have to carry on with the story, you know. I thought you'd appreciate a glimpse into a murderer's sex life, his innermost thoughts.

My God. You don't care about any of this. You're getting bored, fine, let's do this properly. I'll ask your questions, you can just sit back, let's get this going, let me do all the work, I've been doing all the work anyway, here, I hope you don't mind my impersonation of you.

—Oh please do tell us about your wife Gwen.

—Oh very well then. She was a lovely little woman, blonde, I

think. Met her at a museum. Found her very attractive, I think I
may have fallen in love with her straight away.

—Museum?

—Yes, a place with... well you know what a museum is,
surely.

—I thought you'd said a bar.

—Bar? No, no, museum. An exhibition. Gauguin perhaps.
Don't remember. I remember the shapes, the very dark but very
empty colors, the potential, yes, Gauguin almost certainly.

—Yes but earlier you said

—Yes I know what I said earlier but

—But you said it was a bar. Did you meet your wife at a bar or
at a Gauguin exhibition?

—Both, both. That's the one. A bar with Gauguin paintings
hanging off the walls, perhaps. A beautiful woman, but not
beautiful according to anyone else. You see that's why I, well, we,
Gwen and I, fell in love. You see. Because I saw her beauty.

—But a bar and a museum are not the

—Enough.

—Yes.

—Very well, a beautiful woman whose beauty I could see and
nobody else could. Blonde I think. Dark blonde. Not a redhead at
any rate. Now I should specify this because it's important, see,
that I find the idea of a beautiful woman very problematic. As a
man. A man who cares, that is, because how can you fall in love
with a woman and yet be indifferent to certain problems too
serious not to contemplate? I mean of course the... oh, I'm trying
to explain it, but naming it will give you the wrong impression. I
said earlier about feminism. How killing her was the ultimate
feminist act. I did say that, didn't I? Perhaps not the ultimate
feminist act, but it was for the Feminist Cause. See I ruined it
when I said that. I should have made it clear I am not a feminist,
mainly because I am not allowed to be.

—Slow down now, let's take this one step at a

—No, no slowing down here, old pal. Certainly no time for that. I'm sweating now. You see what this does to me. It's not guilt, I did the right thing. It was the correct thing to do. But, well, it leaves me conflicted. Let's keep talking about Gwen: it's like this, she's a good example of it. She was a woman. Biologically. Well, biologically she was a thing, not a woman, let's not give it a precise name. Because when you call her woman, you're already changing her. Call her a thing first. She was, first and foremost, just there. Then because of various factors, we can skip them maybe, no time to go into a history of the entire human world, but, yes, because of certain factors she was determined by us, that is, not-Gwen, that her vagina determined her brain. See now. That's how it works, isn't it.

—Yes well yes but

—But nothing, that's how this is. But I promise you, I'm not going the direction you probably think I'm going. I don't care about social equality. There is no room for that in my world. I'm not indignant about the plight of Woman as a Thing. Don't care. Really, truly, if I am a good feminist, it is because I don't care.

—At all?

—I don't care.

—In that case why do you call yourself... well why a feminist in any case?

—Because instead of outrage, instead of impatience, I feel only an intellectual curiosity, as far as feminism is concerned. And let me tell you, I agree with a good deal of the brighter things feminists say. I am going to come across as insane when you write me up, fine, okay, but I am a progressive liberal, also. With elitist tendencies perhaps. But I put those aside. I think.

—Yes...

—Oh let me put it this way. I see very well the injustice of the world, we all do, those of us who qualify as human. It is a situation of inequality. Yes. But I don't care about equality. If I'm a feminist it's because I find the plight of women more interesting than the plight of men. It's an intellectual exercise. You see? You root for the underdog or you're going to get bored. I welcome the destruction of the patriarchy, although that word bores me too. Patriarchy! Paranoid word. It's absolutely correct, of course, in certain cases. But generally, no, patriarchy as a concept doesn't sit well with me. It's too all-encompassing. These are my thoughts on feminism. Let's move on.

—But you were saying about

—No, I was saying about Gwen. Gwen was a good example of all of this because she wouldn't leave the house without her makeup. I only realized this by the time we were in love, and I had to look past the problem. She had to wear her makeup. Not a great deal of it, but enough. Cover imaginary blemishes. How aggravating, and for a hundred million reasons, too. Who do you need to impress? Who else matters if we're leaving the house together? Who's going to judge you? How can you possibly think you are an independent human being like this? How dare you pretend to have any confidence at all? How can I tell you I love you when I am looking at your face as seeing your insecurities painted all over your cheeks? Why have you stopped believing that I am attracted to you? How can you possibly have a job and a mortgage and still lack the courage to show your perfectly lovely face without going to the bathroom first and painting it? Where am I going to find my respect for you? And I know these sound like harsh overreactions.

—They could be construed that way. Do you mean all of it?

—Of course I do. Listen. How do you convince the woman you love that she's fine as she is? Nobody ever feels fine as they are. What am I going to say to her? Hey Gwen: Out of the billions of rotten things walking upright on this ball of despair, I suspect only fifty are in any way beautiful, thirty have understood the hideous conditions in which we are doomed to progress, and ten genuinely care about someone or something else. These numbers are approximations, my dear, but there is likely to be a very, very small margin of error. I don't believe I have met any of these remarkable individuals but I'm sure they exist, I have no doubt; firstly, because all the legends spread like cancer throughout the generations must have some basis in reality, or I'll kill myself; and secondly, because it seems impossible that out of so many failed experiments in humanity one or two attractive people could not have been produced through chance. Given all this, please accept that although I cannot call you the most beautiful woman on earth, and I don't consider you the most intelligent either, it is not your fault, because I haven't met anyone more beautiful...

— You make little sense.

— You know, when I hear myself speaking I wonder whose voice I'm hearing. My mind is going wrong, I have a rotting head, fixed firmly on my neck and speaking and blinking, and so on, doing everything a head should do. Hair, light and curly, almost white really, I have that, I look human, my head is just like this. That's how a head looks, and if you look me in the eyes, you probably think I'm doing very well, that I'm healthy, at least physically, you think I'm looking back at you. The truth is I don't think this is my head. It feels wrong. I recognize my thoughts, and my memories, and even the voice inside me that speaks to imaginary people. I do not recognize the head itself. It feels too heavy, too clumsy. Someone must have removed my head, emptied out its contents, and placed everything that was once my private world into a new head, not sure when that happened. Now this new head is sitting on my neck, and there is no way to verify that it's really mine, since when I look in the mirror I see only the face I've grown used to over the years.

— What am I meant to... make of that?

— Nothing, that was for your readers.

— But surely you

— No, no, you have to understand that I am quite sincere occasionally, but I realize you need soundbites for your headlines. I have all sorts of sensational things I like to do, and being quotable is one of them. Also your readers will want to know what our marriage was like. I was unfaithful! What do you think our marriage was like? From the moment Gwen and I were married I knew I would be unfaithful, but I couldn't stand the idea that maybe she was cheating on me, too. All it took was that kiss at the altar, well, that metaphorical altar, since there was no ceremony, that horrible moment when the world watched as I put my lips to hers and was pronounced husband till death, for me to realize I no longer loved her the way I once had.

—I suppose you wish to speak about it.

—Yes. Because marriage is just that. It was like this: looking my best, forced to enjoy the most beautiful day of my life, expected by my ghosts to think only of my wife and of our happy future together: I couldn't help but imagine taking someone else from behind. And yes, I felt guilty, though the guilt, I might specify, didn't feel like it belonged to me. Does that make sense? I was harboring someone else's guilt, because to me, it seemed natural that I should want to fuck someone else on my wedding day. In fact I don't think it could have gone any other way. If you can honestly say that marriage has made you want to be faithful, then I tip my hat to you and you may go away, because the rest of us have to deal with these enormous surges of lust that won't go away no matter how many times you get home late after a "work meeting" or "traffic jam"...

—You're monstrously honest.

—Yes, but my main problem isn't my infidelity, because the guilt I feel when I'm spreading someone's legs doesn't feel like it belongs to me; it simply hovers above me, like a cloud that could melt into rain or could not, depending on patterns far beyond my powers of understanding. It's a cloud that just happens to be there when I'm cheating, and I'm not convinced that it's an effect of the cheating itself. No, my problem is my jealousy. I'm doomed. I am introspective to a fault. I know myself, I think, I hope, I know why I feel what I feel; the stupid thing is that I can't seem to change myself. I know very well that I only fucked other women because I was terrified that Gwen was doing the same. Or rather, maybe it's that I was terrified Gwen was fucking other men because I was fucking other women. The point is that I love and hate women, I love the smell and the taste. Breasts are beautiful when they're small, when they're big, it doesn't really matter to me. They're perfect, each in its own way. And so my jealous mind at once tells me that my wife loves to guzzle cock that isn't mine. Now that drives me insane.

—This is in stark contrast to your earlier pronouncements...

—I'm not sure I know what you mean. Gwen was my favorite. I liked to see my ejaculate slide out of her cunt and down her legs. Therefore, by the logic of jealousy, Gwen must have enjoyed having semen rolling out of her. Which made me want to beat her, though I've never even slapped anyone. Well, apart from the incident with the strangulation. I'm not a violent guy, not physically. Maybe inside there are breezes of discontent but my anger never translates into violence, unless the violence is sexual. Oh yes. I like to fuck you as though you just killed my family. And you like it too, or you wouldn't let me do it. Jesus.

—Perhaps if we

—Nope.

—Nope... but

—No, no, we're still talking about, no, we aren't even.

—After a long shower wetter with dread than with water, I dressed and left the house. So I said: "Let me ask you something. But... I'd like to get to know you first."

—Then we went quiet again.

—Her name was April and she had a mole on her neck and I found it charming. This was surprising. And moles are never really part of who you are; I have a mole on my back and if you removed it with scissors, I'd be more upset over the pain than over losing the mole.. She grunted, and she squirmed, and she said, "Yes," and I thought: Isn't this supposed to be about me?

—But that was a stupid thought to have, and I realized it at once. "So," she said.

—I knew very well that if I simply ordered her to undress and spread her legs, she would do it; it was in the job description, and she expected nothing more from me. To speed things along, I'll just tell you what happened once I was alone with April in a room. Perfect square little teeth; I imagined them clicking together in the cold and making a pleasantly dry sound. The problem was that I needed to feel some kind of sympathy from her. I should specify that I never discovered exactly whose room it was. I wanted to kiss it because I knew it must have caused her some shame. You want to know about the prostitute.

—But it wasn't a sexual thought. Since then I've learned that April was a particularly excitable woman, and not everyone becomes quite so wet, but, having had no experience before that day, I felt a mild disgust, as though I'd seen someone blow their nose. I said: "You study?"

—Study? No. It wasn't hard for me to spend hours scribbling in Latin on the wall behind my bed. I'd heard about it, of course; but I hadn't expected it to be so, well, wet. Still, she smiled, and I took off my jeans and touched her breasts. Little idealist that I was, there was no hope of getting an erection if all I knew about her was her name and the location of a mole. Anyway, on my eighteenth birthday my father gave me some money and told me to spend it wisely. I'll skip the details, but I want to mention one thing about discovering the feminine wetness. She was smiling. I like silence but that was a terrible moment. Her eyes blinked only sometimes. So I decided to lose my virginity once and for all, as all virginities must be lost, and I remembered April.

—The streets around here have been cleaned up nicely, there is no blood anywhere, the corpses are gone, the debris is gone, the smell of death is elsewhere for a while, I have to be careful not to use a full stop in public, people notice and rat on you, that's the state of things, what can you do — today it is as though no riot had ever taken place in this city — overnight it seems the rubble was removed and the people around me keep on going as usual, men are wearing business suits again and carrying briefcases, the ones with office jobs — an office job is the best kind you can get, you don't have to worry about anything except your job, the tyrant leaves you alone mostly, I hear you can even be exempt from certain legal obligations — you don't have to worry about the full stops, for instance, because every office job in this country relates back to increasing the tyrant's hold on us, you have to use periods in your documents to show how above the law you seem to be — so if you work in an office, you dress nicely, you stagger your speech, you carry all sorts of fancy punctuation around in your pockets and nobody searches you, and the whole deal with the government is that you help solidify the tyrant's tyranny by making every legal document intended for the public as incomprehensible and irrelevant as you can — that is, you have to make it impossible for the untrained reader or, in other words, the average person to understand just what the hell any particular document is saying — and they don't hide that from you, either — everyone knows this is how things work — occasionally you can find someone, what they call a jargon reader, who, for a slightly elevated fee, will interpret what a given document is trying to communicate — untangle the syntax, simplify the language, rearrange certain phrases, take out all the needless preliminary stuff — so that if, for example, you're handed a fine that you can't understand, you could, in theory, find a jargon reader and pay him to tell you what the fine says — the problem is that jargon reading is illegal, because it's an act of terroristic translation, as they call it, so it's hard to find a good jargon reader who's both discreet and trustworthy — after all, you could make any old shit up and call yourself a jargon reader — but anyway — none of this really matters — I need to decide… I need to decide what I'm going to do — do I go to X and meet this bitch — do I run away — do I kill myself — the streets are so clean, so attractive, there is sunlight, more and more people are venturing out, someone is walking a dog, you don't see dogs very often — I'm dressed in a suit that fits me perfectly, a strange thing to happen, a beige suit, white shirt just right, brown tie to hang myself with, comfortable shoes that are exactly my size, everything's just great — Y, I assume, took my measurements while I was unconscious — or he's been following me and trying to pass our meeting off as coincidence — but that's unlikely — well, nothing's very likely — in this suit, the coziest, the most wonderful thing I have worn in years, I feel empowered — stupid but effective — he's trying to buy me — win me over to his cause — he wants me to meet this bitch and slowly grow committed to the fighting — by the time I return and tell him what she wants I'll feel like I'm helping in the struggle for freedom — manipulative bastard — who even knows if this bitch isn't in fact just an actress he's hired — but that makes no sense — or only some sense — there is nothing so special about me that could warrant such measures... The buses are running again, I take the 74 towards Belle Grave Street, which is two minutes away from X according to Y's instructions, I take a seat — I keep thinking about my hair — it's the dumbest thing, but whenever I catch a glimpse of myself in a mirror or, in this case, a reflection in the bus window, I suddenly realize — as I did for the first time this morning and many times since — that Y shaved the back of my head so he could stitch me up — fair enough — but he left some hair near my temples and on my scalp, as though he couldn't be bothered to finish the job — result is I look mentally handicapped, in a fancy beige suit and patches of hair around my head, with no doubt a glazed look in my eyes from the drugs he put me on — but I feel fine and maybe that is all.

√ good work

PERFECT
EDGE
BOOKS

We live in uncertainty. New ways of committing crimes are discovered every day. Hackers and hit men are idolized. Writers have responded to this either by ignoring the harsher realities or by glorifying mindless violence for the sake of it. Atrocities (from the Holocaust to 9/11) are exploited in cheaply sentimental films and novels.

Perfect Edge Books proposes to find a balanced position. We publish fiction that doesn't revel in nihiliom, doesn't go for gore at the cost of substance — yet we want to confront the world with its beauty as well as its ugliness. That means we want books about difficult topics, books with something to say.

We're open to dark comedies, "transgressive" novels, potboilers and tales of revenge. All we ask is that you don't try to shock for the sake of shocking — there is too much of that around. We are looking for intelligent young authors able to use the written word for changing how we read and write in dark times.